Best Slayed Plans

A Poppy Lewis Mystery

Book 2

Lucinda Harrison

Best Slayed Plans

Copyright © 2021 by Lucinda Harrison

All rights reserved. No part of this publication may be reproduced, distributed, or transmitted in any form or by any means, including photocopying, recording, or other electronic or mechanical methods without the prior written permission of the copyright holder, except in the case of brief quotations in critical reviews and certain other noncommercial uses permitted by copyright law.

This is a work of fiction. Names, characters, places, and incidents are either the product of the author's imagination or are used fictitiously, and any resemblance to actual persons, living or dead, business establishments, events, or locales is entirely coincidental.

ISBN: 978-1-7367596-1-5

*To my best furry friends, Buddy and LuLu,
who make life interesting every day.*

One

"WHY ISN'T THIS working?" I grumbled to the renovation gods as I tried twisting the lightbulb into the socket. I perched on the top of the ladder, trying to reach the high ceiling of the Victorian mansion's foyer. A lock of my black hair had come loose from my ponytail and fallen into my eyes. With no hands free, I blew it away from my face with a quick puff and flick of my head.

"You're doing it wrong," Harper said, scoffing.

"I know how it works."

"Then why isn't it working?" She stood on the floor holding the base of the ladder with her thin dark hands, watching me struggle with this simple task. A rainbow scarf wrapped around her forehead, allowing her tight brown curls to emerge out of the top like a mushroom. "Righty-tighty, lefty-loosey."

"Need some help?" a voice asked from the open doorway.

A slender woman leaned against the door frame, grinning at the two of us. She held her straight black hair back with a red kerchief and blue coveralls clashed with her long-sleeved striped work shirt. A hint of tattoos peeked out at the wrist and collar, giving her an overall sense of quiet self-assurance.

"Thanks, Cho," I said. "I don't know what I'm doing wrong." I inched my way down the ladder and let Cho ascend. She flew up without a second thought until she was at the top.

"Make sure the switch is off," Cho said. I checked that it was off and in no time she secured the new bulb and we were all three back on the wooden floor. "There you go. Next time be sure to remove the light bulb safety cover I installed on all the plugs and sockets. These wires are old, and I take no chances."

"Harper," I said, "this is Cho. She's the electrician working on the renovations."

Harper held out a hand to Cho and beamed a megawatt smile. "Pleased to meet you."

Cho returned her smile and greeting and added an almost imperceptible head tilt. Her dark eyes twinkling. "I like your headband," she said. "I've only been on site a few days. Do you come around often?"

Harper nodded, her expanse of hair bobbing along above the headband. "Every day except Sundays." Harper spread her arms wide and twirled to expose the full effect of her Postal Service uniform then shot a thumb back at me. "Poppy stopped me this time to hold the ladder so she could flop around in her hopeless attempt to install a simple lightbulb."

I rolled my eyes. "Neither of us knew about the plugs."

Harper added, "I'm sure there's a hilarious joke in

there somewhere about how many friends it takes to screw in a lightbulb, but it's escaping me at the moment."

A voice called a greeting from the open doorway and we all turned to see Angie Owens, Starry Cove's resident baker, trudging up the walkway through the rain. "Ahoy there, ladies. Thought I'd sail over through this rain and bring some coffee. And I suspected Harper would be here, too." A few lines crinkled at the corner of her eyes, which twinkled at correctly predicting Harper's location. Her chubby cheeks puffed out as a satisfied grin spread across her face.

"Thanks Angie," I said, taking the coffee carrier from her as she stepped out of the rain and took off her dripping coat and shook a bit of water from her short brown hair. I grabbed one coffee out of the carrier and handed it to Harper. "You always know just what we need."

"Oh, sorry," said Angie, eyeing Cho. "I only brought three."

"Don't worry," said Cho, holding up a dismissive hand. "I've already had coffee, thanks."

"Angie, this is Cho—" My arm swept toward Cho but bumped the entry way table and my coffee slipped to the floor, dumping hot steaming brew across the floorboards. "Shoot."

"I'll grab some towels," said Cho, heading off through the plastic divider that separated the foyer from the kitchen. She returned a few moments later, and we all ripped off a few sheets and began sopping up the liquid.

"Sorry," said Harper. I glanced over, thinking Harper was talking to me, but saw her and Cho sharing flushed smiles after brushing hands reaching for a towel.

"Cho," came a booming voice from the kitchen.

"Where are you? I know you're here somewhere."

"I'm in the entryway, Blister. Calm down." Cho shook her head and shared a sardonic grin with the rest of us as we stood up, floor cleaned and now infused with the scent of coffee—which I'd consider an improvement.

Bill "Blister" Hauser, burly lumberjack of a man, burst through the plastic seal into the foyer. Towering over six-feet tall, Blister filled the doorway as he passed through. He was a working man—his khaki work pants had about a thousand pockets and a pencil stuck out from his ball cap, tucked above an ear. His blue shirt was covered in gypsum dust from the drywall. Mud from something outside smeared across his pants as though he'd used them as a towel.

"Oh," he said, staring down at us. "There's more of you. Nice to see you again, Harper." He turned to Cho and held up a handful of what looked like plastic noodles. "I can't figure out this bundle of wires."

"You shouldn't be figuring out any bundles of wires in this rain. You know that."

"Right," he said, shoving them into the back pocket of his work pants.

"Blister," Angie called out, worming her way to the front of the pack of women. "What are you doing here?"

"Angie," he said, surprised. "How have you been?"

"You already know Blister?" I asked.

"I sure do. He's my cousin. Well, he's my second cousin. Our moms were cousins. I think." Angie stared off, trying to figure out the connection in her head.

"That's right," said Blister. "Angie's like a little sister. Haven't seen you in a while, though. I've been working a lot in Vista and haven't been to Starry Cove in, oh, I can't remember how long."

"Too long," Angie said. "That's how long."

"I still remember this mansion, though," he said. "Big purple monster greeting everyone who came into town. Angie and I used to think it was haunted."

Angie's cheeks reddened. "Only a little when we were really young."

"I appreciate these types of houses more now. Excellent example of a classic Queen Anne Victorian. Not sure about the color, but Poppy here"—he gestured to me—"insisted we keep it purple."

"To honor Arthur, my late uncle," I clarified for Cho. "He painted the house this color when he bought it. I inherited it from him and moved here just a few months ago."

"I see you've all met Cho," he said. "She's our electrician, but you should come around and meet the rest of the crew. They're quite a cast of characters."

***

Harper and Angie followed Blister and me into the dining room, which I'd rarely used since moving into the house. The space was enormous, much too large as a dining room for just me. High ceilings gave the room a stately appearance and a medallion in the center looked bare where a large crystal chandelier used to hang—I'd taken it down before renovations and had plans to use it elsewhere. The space was now being revamped into a room that would accommodate multiple diners. That's why I was suffering through renovations, after all. Eventually, this big gorgeous mansion would be the best and brightest bed-and-breakfast in the county. But I needed Blister and his crew to turn my vision into reality.

Two men occupied the dining room when we crowded in with all the gear and equipment.

"Edgar, Quentin. Have you met my cousin, Angie? And this is Harper."

Edgar grunted from the corner, drill clutched in his hand. He was a colossal statue of sawdust and grime and dwarfed Quentin, who was thinner and more diminutive with mousy hair cut short. Edgar's eyes glared out from underneath his ball cap like dark hollows in an old tree.

"Please to meet you both," said Quentin, smiling.

"These are my carpenters, Edgar Biggs and Quentin…" Blister scratched his head, struggled to pull Quentin's last name.

"Qualls. I do all kinds of construction," said Quentin. "Houses, decks, sheds. You name it."

Edgar sucked through his teeth and cocked his head toward the crooked frame of a pony wall. "Fix that framing, Quentin. It's awful." He leveled his eyes in Blister's direction. "Rain's getting worse. The moisture's messing with my wood."

This Edgar guy was a gruff sort—he was even shorter with me than when I'd met him yesterday. I felt bad for poor Quentin, who was Edgar's apprentice, doomed to spend his days side-by-side taking Edgar's insults and orders like an overworked donkey.

"Well, you guys seem busy," said Blister. "Let's move on."

Blister guided us into the living room, where we found a man holding a sheet of drywall against the insulated framing of the wall. The pop of his nail gun peppered our ears as it drilled nails at high power into the chalky board.

Blister stepped up, waiting for the nail gun pops to end, and tapped him on the shoulder. The man turned around, removing the goggles on his sweaty face. He slid them to the top of his head, like a pair of oversized sunglasses, causing his dark brown hair to stick up at odd angles. He stared bewildered at the group of four standing in front of him.

"Dimitri," said Blister. "This is my cousin, Angie, and her friend Harper. You've met Poppy already."

Angie waved a plump little arm and Harper nodded a greeting in his direction.

"Hello," Dimitri replied. Even with just one word, his eastern-European accent was heavy and thick.

"Dimitri does drywall. He'll be very busy on this big house since we'll be replacing most of it down here on the first floor at least."

"I try to keep history," said Dimitri. "Salvage what possible."

"Then we'll replace the damaged historic wallpaper with a similar motif," I said. "To keep with the style."

Dimitri nodded.

"Let's head to the kitchen next," said Blister. "Thanks Dimitri, we won't bother you anymore."

We trudged into the kitchen single file, following Blister on his trail of introductions. The kitchen had seen the most action since renovations began. Arthur's kitchen, although renovated before, was already out-of-date and needed some serious attention.

As we entered, Angie cried out, "Oh my, it's stripped to the bone."

She called it right—the kitchen was nothing more

than dust and studs, with barely the hint of what used to be there. I needed the kitchen revamped, not just because I'd be hosting future guests who would no doubt expected breakfast during their bed-and-breakfast stay, but because I longed to cook. Well, learn to cook. I wasted many years with a husband who ate nothing but boring meat and potatoes, but once I was free, I let my culinary flag fly. Of course, there were some bumps in the road—don't ask Angie about shrimp linguini—but as soon as the kitchen was done, I planned to invest time in perfecting this new craft.

"Maisie," Blister announced, "is our plumber. Now, you need a good plumber in these old houses—never know what kind of mess you'll find behind these walls."

"No kidding," Harper mumbled. Angie and I shared a meaningful look. We'd had some experience already with things behind walls.

Maisie extracted herself from under the sink, set down her wrench, and slapped her hands on her knees. "Howdy."

Even through the dust cloud Maisie was a pretty woman, with an abundance of strawberry blonde hair wrapped up in a messy bun on top of her head. She wore a headlamp which shined in our faces as she greeted us. I assumed she was around thirty, but with all the grease and grime, she could be older or younger.

"Maisie, this is my cousin, Angie." Blister gestured toward stout little Angie. "And this is Harper. They're friends of Poppy's. I'm giving them the tour of the site."

"Exciting stuff," said Maisie emotionless. "You know these pipes are terrible, Blister. I should charge more for this type of work. The hazards alone—"

"Right," said Blister, chuckling, and ushered us out the kitchen door and onto the back porch. "Let's move on to meet our last two crew members. Quite a pair."

Crashing and cursing came from the back of the house as we rounded the corner of the porch, safely out of the rain. Two men chucked a large piece of plywood into the huge dumpster that had taken up residence on the property. I hadn't met these two before.

"Dustin and Justin. Twins, if you can believe it. They do the labor bit—demo, hauling, that sort of thing."

"You going to make us stay out here, Blister?" one of them shouted.

"Since when did a little rain hurt so bad?" Blister shot back.

The two grumbled and turned back to their work, throwing chunks of wood with increased enthusiasm—or anger.

"Well, I'll leave them be," he said. "We don't want to go out there in the mud, anyway."

"And what do you do around here, Blister? Anything?" asked Angie.

"Me?" he asked, feigning offense. "I'm the general contractor. I keep the rest of these kids in line. And on target."

Just then, the lights streaming through the windows and onto the porch flickered, then went out completely.

Maisie shouted from the kitchen, "Blister, get in here."

Our little group hustled back through the kitchen door, following Blister as he barreled inside.

"What's the matter?" he asked.

"Power's out again."

"Where's Cho?" Blister asked, looking around. "Cho?" he cried out. No response.

"She already left," said Maisie, disappointed.

"All right, no lights, no power, heavy rain. I'm just going to call it a day. Let's pack up and try again tomorrow." Blister turned to me and said, "Sorry, Poppy. This day's a wash."

I shrugged. "It happens."

***

Harper, Angie, and I left the house behind to allow the crew to clean up for the day and headed to Angie's bakery down the street. The rain had let up only a little, so we were happy to reach the dry overhang of her shop's front entry. We shook out our umbrellas and popped into the shop.

"It's just me and the girls," Angie shouted to the back kitchen. Roy, Angie's husband, would be back there, I was sure, tending the shop while Angie came over to check out the house. "Do we have any hot coffee made?" No response. "He can't hear me, probably has his headphones in. I wonder how many customers came in and left without service."

"In this rain?" Harper wondered.

"Yeah, you're probably right. Anyway, I'll put some on." Angie shuffled behind the counter and filled the coffeemaker with grounds.

"I'm glad some work is getting done on the house," said Harper. "I know you wanted to get started as soon as possible. Too bad about the weather."

"There'll be sunnier days to come," said Angie. "I can't believe Blister is your contractor. That's just too funny. He and I used to cause so much trouble." Angie's mind wandered off, and she chuckled at an unspoken memory.

"He came highly recommended," I said. "And he got the crew assembled pretty fast, which was nice."

"Rough, though, weren't they?" asked Harper. "Cho and Quentin seemed to be the only nice ones out of the lot."

"I think they're frustrated from the rain, and the power outages—that wasn't the first—and it doesn't seem like anyone wants to work on a house this old except Blister."

Angie brought over two plates of cinnamon rolls from behind the counter and set them on the small table where Harper and I sat. "These should warm you up."

"You're incredible, thanks," Harper said.

I nodded in agreement. "You really are the best baker I've ever known."

Angie beamed and walked over to a shiny trophy displayed in the front window with pies and cakes and other treats. She gave it a spiff with a clean towel and looked both ways out the rainy window. "Thanks, I just wish today wasn't so stormy. Things have been picking up—I'm even thinking of hiring staff so Roy and I can take a moment away from the bakery to breathe."

"That's a big step," I said. "Is business that good?"

"It's great. My name is getting around, so that leads to more business. I can't complain."

"Well, I think you work entirely too much," said Harper. "That's what I like about my job—the hours are, uh, flexible."

Angie came around and was pouring coffee for the

three of us when the door chimed and Mayor Jim Thornen walked in with a stack of wet flyers in hand. "Good morning ladies," he said, dripping all over the floor. "Glad to find some folks up and out today in this weather."

"And what are you doing?" Harper eyed the papers he held.

"I was walking by and thought our new resident might want to hear about our upcoming election. I'll be running for a third term as Starry Cove's very own mayor, and I hope I can count on your vote, Miss Lewis."

Before I could answer, Harper asked, "What's in it for her?"

Mayor Jim bristled. "I have been a stalwart representative of this town for two terms."

"I'm not so sure. There've been some pretty unsettling events recently on your watch. That's a rough record."

"Harper..." Angie warned in a soft voice.

Mayor Jim crossed his arms, the papers still dripping. "I'll have you know that was Deputy Todd Newman's *watch*, not mine."

Harper rolled her eyes.

"Clearly, Miss Tillman isn't interested, but I've got a flyer for both of you." He handed Angie and I each a soggy page from the stack.

I read the header out loud, "Vote for Thornen—More of the Same." Mayor Jim's face beamed out from the center of the flyer, but the ink now ran in rivulets down the page, melting his face into the figure in The Scream.

"Catchy," I said.

"I'm running unopposed, but it's still important to

make the effort—come out and see the people, you know. I'm here for any questions if you have them." He waited a moment, but no one spoke up. "Well, I'll let you ladies enjoy your meal." He sauntered out of the bakery and popped open his umbrella before making a sharp turn out of sight.

"Stalwart representative," Harper mocked. "What a dolt. That man couldn't lead his way out of a kiddie maze."

A few moments later the bakery door chimed open and Lovie Newman, wife of the town's deputy sheriff, entered with a cheery smile. "I saw the mayor leave and thought I'd pop over and grab one of your delicious muffins, Angie."

Angie beamed. "Thanks, Lovie. They're in the case, take a look."

"Why'd you wait for the mayor to leave?" asked Harper, a sly smile touching her lips. I shook my head but said nothing. Not too long ago, I'd caught Lovie and Mayor Jim in an affair, but no one was supposed to know. I *may* have accidentally shared that bit of information with Angie and Harper.

Lovie spun around to the case. "I have no idea what you mean. Why, these look scrumptious."

Angie hustled behind the counter to bag the muffins. "Mayor Jim was just telling us about the upcoming election."

"Oh? Yes, I suppose he would be. You know, he's running unopposed again."

"So he said," Harper drawled, still unimpressed with anything about Mayor Jim.

"Thanks, Angie," Lovie said, taking the bag. She

turned back to Harper and me. "Barely anyone bothered to show up to vote last time. I think he got a total of twenty out of the whole township. But, since there were no other candidates, twenty was enough."

"Twenty?" Harper gagged. "Only twenty people bothered to vote for him?"

Lovie nodded. "That's right. Now, I probably shouldn't have shared that with you three, but I know you'll be discreet." She headed to the door, pulling her hood over her coiffed blonde-gray curls. "Bye ladies," she said, disappearing into the rain.

"Why don't *you* run for mayor?" I asked Harper. "He's running unopposed."

Angie clapped and her eyes lit up. "That's a great idea."

Harper scoffed. "No way. I love my freedom too much and it's hard being nice to people all the time."

"Oh," Angie nodded. "You do struggle with that." She headed to the window and peered out once again. "Looks like the rain's dying down now."

"Great," Harper said, "I've got to get back to my route."

"And I need to get back to the house. Everyone will be gone by now and I'm hoping Blister has the electricity back on."

***

With the rain letting up, I walked back toward the house. The glorious old mansion sat on the edge of a roundabout at the entry into town, and there was no way to miss it driving in. Even now, with the mist still lingering, it loomed over the land in all its purple glory. Despite beginning renovations, I had every intent to keep as much of the outside charm—and inside—as possible. The old place was practically a landmark around these parts, partly due to its grandeur and partly due to the vibrant paint job.

An arched trellis led up from the sidewalk to the front porch and I dipped underneath, trying to dodge the residual drips from the clematis that hung heavy on its frame. Blister was on the front porch, wrapping a cord around some tool or another, and I approached him with a smile.

"Hey Blister, everyone head out already?"

"Yep, just me left. Your power's back on, by the way."

"Thanks, I'm going to head upstairs to change. Would you lock it on your way out?"

"Sure thing. I've got just a few things to pack up and I'll be off myself. A big fat orange cat wandered in earlier—I wasn't sure if it was yours or not, so I didn't flush it out. He looked pretty soaked."

"No worries, that's just Mayor Dewey trying to get out of the rain." Mayor Dewey, the town's resident cat, often made his way to the big house as it was one of his favorite spots to lounge and watch the world go by. He was not a mayor of anything—it was a title Harper applied long ago as a dig at Mayor Jim, and it seemed to have stuck.

I began climbing the stairway that led up from the foyer to the rooms above before I noticed my shoes were leaving wet prints in my wake. Stopping on the switchback landing, I steadied myself on the sturdy rails and took them off, carrying them in my hands, before continuing to the second floor. A large landing space led off to separate bedrooms, each to become its own suite once the renovations were complete.

My soggy shoes continued to drip, so I stepped to the bathroom located around the back of the stairwell opening. The door was ajar, and I nudged it open with my hip and dropped the shoes on the tiled floor, where they could dry. As I headed back out the doorway, my pants caught on something, tugging me backward. Looking down to free myself, I noticed the doorknob and door jamb were ripped and broken from the framing. I cursed Blister's crew and promised to bring it up tomorrow once Blister arrived at the house.

For now, I wanted to change out of my wet clothes and into something warm. I love the rain, and nothing makes me happier than snuggling up with a hot cup of coffee in cozy pajamas and listening to the rain fall—all from a safe, dry location. I kept one room upstairs as my own for the time being, until the final renovations were complete, and I could add a small wing downstairs for my private residence. For now, the belongings from my old life pre-Starry Cove filled the smallest of the rooms upstairs.

I grabbed a set of cozy pink pajamas from the dresser and changed. I carried my previous clothes to the closet where I kept my hamper and opened the door to throw them in, wet and all—I'd do laundry tomorrow—but as I eased the door open, a most gruesome and unexpected sight filled my vision. There, slumped against the hamper, lay Edgar Biggs, eyes bulging and unmoving, tongue protruding from his blank face. A large rivulet of blood ran down his face from a single nail driven into the middle of his forehead, like the rain dripping down my bedroom windowpane.

I fell back and stumbled, shocked, wet clothes still in my hands. The cinnamon roll and coffee from earlier threatened to come back up as I scrambled to my feet and rushed out the door. I shouted for Blister as I faltered down the steps, hoping he might still be on site.

He dashed through the front door and spotted me drooped on the stairwell. The look on my face must have spurred him to action, since he rushed over to grab me before I fell the rest of the way down the stairs.

"What's wrong?" he asked, holding me upright.

I couldn't speak. The moment caught like a rope around my throat.

"Poppy, tell me what's wrong."

"Edgar—" was all I could muster as I tried to catch my breath.

"What about Edgar?"

"He's dead!"

Two

"A-YUP, NAIL GUN to the head." Sheriff's Deputy Todd Newman stood just outside the entryway with his walkie-talkie in hand. "Shot point-blank. We found him in a closet." I didn't know who he was talking to, but he didn't seem too fazed by what was going on around him. His wiry frame made him seem slight and unassuming, perhaps weak. For those who didn't know Deputy Todd, he was just a small-town deputy sheriff, but for me, he was a tolerated necessity—an oft-appearing pebble in my proverbial shoe.

It started raining again as I sat on a bench on the wrap-around porch with a blanket draped over me. The nights were chilly on the coast, but I would have rather been outside than in the house at that moment. Mayor Dewey, the big ginger cat, lay curled in my lap, like an oversized mug of coffee warming me when I needed it the most.

A small car pulled up and parked along the roundabout—the medical team and sheriff's vehicles had taken up the entire driveway. It was Angie's car, and I was thankful to see her and Harper hop out and run up the wet walkway to my side.

"Oh, Poppy," Angie said through her tears as she wrapped her arms around me.

"I can't believe this is happening again." Harper sat down next to me. "Are you all right?"

"I don't know. The shock of it…" I didn't want to relive it, and my friends understood. I'd had a similar experience not too long ago, and the events had shaken me. I guess this type of thing doesn't get easier with practice.

Deputy Todd finished his conversation and strolled up to our little group. "Ladies," he said, tipping his oversized hat toward Harper and Angie. "Regretful that we're meeting again under these circumstances." His voice was slow and drawled out, as though irritated that these events had put a dampener on his day.

"Deputy," called a voice through the rain. It was Mayor Jim, half-running down the sidewalk toward the house. Harper rolled her eyes.

Deputy Todd shot us a quick look. "I'll take care of this." He stepped off the porch to intercept the mayor. There was no love lost between these two, and their egos were both sore over it. I promised Deputy Todd I wouldn't say anything about what happened between his wife, Lovie, and the mayor since he and I shared a similar betrayal from the one person we each should have trusted the most—our spouse.

"Now, Deputy, what's this here? I saw the lights and the cars and such and I demand to know what's going on in *my* town."

Lucinda Harrison

"Be quiet, Jim," Deputy Todd snapped. "There's been a murder, and it's being investigated by the *authorities*. If I have any questions about pageants or sidewalk improvements, I'll let you know."

Mayor Jim bristled. "Now just you wait a minute—"

"Until then, I'll have to ask you to leave."

"But what about them?" He waved a hand in our direction.

"Miss Lewis lives here, or have you forgotten?"

"What about the other two?"

"Mind your business, Mayor. Now, skedaddle before I arrest you for trespassing at a crime scene during an investigation."

Mayor Jim's fiery expression faded. "Fine," he said, pointing a finger at the deputy. "But I'll remind you that an election is coming up, and this town needs safety and security—I just hope you're up for it." And with that, the mayor stomped away, leaving Deputy Todd standing on the walkway, a waterfall of rain pouring off the brim of his hat.

"Nuisance," the deputy mumbled and turned back to the house, steam boiling out of his ears. He stepped back onto the porch and shouted into the house, "I want to talk to Blister Hauser right now."

Soon enough, Blister appeared on the porch, his face full of worry. His eyes were red, as though he'd been crying, and he stood silently with his hands in the pockets of his work pants.

"Blister, you've already been interviewed, but can you think of anything more—anything—that could lead us to who murdered Edgar Biggs?"

"Sorry, Deputy. I've already told you guys what I

know. I didn't see anyone come into the house, and I can't believe anyone on my crew could have done anything like this."

Angie piped up from the sidelines, "You must have seen something Blister, tell them."

"I didn't, Angie. After the crew left, I walked to the hardware store down the street to pick up some things for tomorrow. Glad I did, too, since Trevor was just closing up his shop."

Deputy Todd pulled out a spiral-bound notebook and scribbled. "So, you weren't here? Do you have any receipts from the store?"

"No sir, I didn't get one. After these ladies left the house, the crew and I packed up and I thought they all left. That's when I went to the store."

"But Edgar didn't leave," I said in a hushed tone.

"No, I suppose he didn't. I can't say I watched them all leave personally, but they were all packing up and knew we were heading out for the day. I don't know what could have happened."

"Poor Edgar," said Angie.

"I'm really sorry for his kids. He'd just got an order for more custody and was looking forward to spending more time with them."

"Oh no…" Angie's face fell, and she started tearing up. "Those poor kids."

"What about the nail gun we found in the closet? You said it belonged to one of your crew."

"That's right, Dimitri."

"What about him?" Deputy Todd pushed. "He has to have some training in use of the thing, right?"

"It's a pretty basic tool, Deputy. You just sort of pick

it up and pull the trigger."

"Wait," said Harper. "Wasn't the power out? How could anyone use a nail gun with no power?"

"It's battery-operated—no cords," said Blister. "We all used it here on site. It's a nice tool, top-of-the-line. Whenever Dimitri didn't have it in his own hand, someone else did, even Edgar."

"Can you think of any reason someone would want to kill him?" I tightened the blanket around me, bracing for the answer.

"Edgar isn't—wasn't—too popular with the crew. Bit of a rough personality."

"I got that impression," said Harper.

"But I wouldn't say anyone could kill him. Maisie was his wife. She would know more about him and his enemies."

My jaw hit the floor. "She's his wife?"

"Was. Ex-wife for a year or so now."

Deputy Todd's brow went up. "Ex-wife, huh? How'd that work out?"

"A job's a job, Deputy. They showed up and got the job done. Kept it civil, you know. Most of these guys worked multiple contracts. She's also working that new shopping center in Vista."

"Is there anything else that seemed odd to you?" I asked. "Anything out of place or strange?"

He thought for a moment "I guess Cho seemed awfully eager to be on the project when she found out Edgar was going to be the carpenter on this big house. But I don't think she could have done this, either."

Deputy Todd sighed. "It seems like you don't think anyone on your crew had the personality to kill Edgar except Edgar."

"I wish I could help more, Deputy."

"It's all right. You can leave, but I want you to stay in communication. This is an open investigation—anyone could be a suspect—so I don't want any of you taking off when no one is looking."

"Understood. Goodnight ladies," he said, nodding our way.

"Oh Blister," Angie wailed, running up to embrace him. Her arms didn't fit around his waist and her head barely reached mid-chest, but he hugged her back before leaving.

***

I didn't want to stay at the house or spend the night there, so Angie offered to let me stay at her place down the road. I'd spent the night there before when I'd first arrived in Starry Cove—electricity issues, coincidentally—and found her little green cottage cozy and inviting. Harper, Angie, and I found ourselves around Angie's dining room table. Angie's husband, Roy, who ran the bakery with her, had retreated to his den to watch some sporting event, leaving us alone and in private.

"I can't believe Blister is even a suspect," said Angie. "He wouldn't hurt a fly."

"He was the last one there, so I can see how it might look to everyone else," I said. "But I agree, he's so kind and gentle, even if he is built like a mountain."

"When we were kids, he always towered over everyone else. He was really self-conscious about it too." Angie leaned back and pulled a photo album from the bookcase behind her. "There're pictures of us in here somewhere." She flipped through and stopped at a page of faded Polaroids that captured the outdoor adventures of two kids—the little girl short, plump, and rosy-cheeked and the boy all gangly limbs and grins.

"This is us on the grass at my old house," Angie said, pointing to the photographs. "I remember Blister—Billy back then—got stung by a bee. He didn't cry when he got stung, but he wailed like a baby when my mom told him that bees die after stinging. Gosh, he felt so bad for that little bee. He just doesn't have it in him to do anything this awful."

"I believe you Angie," I said.

"Me too," said Harper, taking up our hands in hers. "Now, what's up with that Maisie lady?"

"That seemed *very* suspicious."

"Who works in close quarters with an ex? That's just asking for trouble."

"I agree," I said. "And I bet Maisie could shed a lot more light on this than Blister could."

Just then my cell phone rang, I pulled it out of my pocket and noticed I had three messages. I didn't recognize the number. "Hello?" I answered.

"Miss Lewis, this is Deputy Todd Newman."

"Oh, Hi Deputy Todd," I said loud enough for the others to hear. Harper and Angie stopped talking at the mention of his name and turned their attention to me.

"Look, Miss Lewis, I'm afraid I'm going to have to shut down your renovation while we investigate Edgar Biggs's murder."

"Shut down the reno?" I cried into the phone. "But I'm on a timeline."

"I understand, but this is an official law enforcement

investigation."

"For how long?"

"Until it's solved, Miss Lewis. You do understand the gravity of the situation, I hope."

"I do," I said with a grumble.

"And it's not looking too good for your general contractor," he added. I tried to muffle his voice so Angie couldn't hear, but he continued, "Blister was the last one at the house, last one to leave, no one else was there. Big, powerful guy. It's all pointing to him, unfortunately."

"I guess I'll let him know the project is on hold."

"I already did," said Deputy Todd. "And I told him to break the news to his crew, so don't expect anyone to show up tomorrow."

"Gee, thanks," I said with a sigh.

"I know what you're thinking, Poppy."

"Oh?"

"Yeah. Stay out of this one. We don't want a repeat of last time, do we?"

"Got it."

I ended the call and stared woefully at Harper and Angie.

"I can't believe that clown is shutting down your reno," said Harper.

"And Blister isn't in the clear, is he?" asked Angie.

"Sorry Angie. Looks like I'm at a standstill and my general contractor is the prime suspect."

Three

THE RAIN STOPPED by the next morning, and Angie and I shared a plate of scones and coffee before she headed to the bakery after Roy, while I trudged reluctantly back to the house.

The first thing I noticed was that it still looked like it was in the middle of a full renovation project. The crew's projects still sat, half-finished in their makeshift workrooms, the sawhorses were still set up in the living room. I'd shoved Arthur's old sofa, which I'd inherited along with the house, against the wall for the time being to make space for the work crew. The entire place looked like a disaster.

I found the nerve to go upstairs to my room, but only to grab some clothes to tide me over for a few days. I had no intention of spending another night in there—not with Edgar's ghost hanging out in my closet. I was surprised how clean everything looked after the medical and sheriff crews had their way with it, but I honestly couldn't remember if blood splattered the place or not—it had taken me so much by surprise. The only thing I remembered was that single nail jutting out of Edgar's bloody forehead. I shivered and headed back downstairs.

Except for my room upstairs, I'd had most of the furniture put into storage, including the magnificent set of Victorian-era gilt furniture that made up one of the bedrooms. I'd cataloged everything before the movers hauled it to the secure storage unit, knowing it had true value and would be an important asset once I opened the bed-and-breakfast. I planned to offer one room billed as a grand Victorian suite, complete with authentic furniture. That was just one surprise Arthur had left me.

The closet downstairs was large enough that I'd shoved my inflatable mattress inside—the one I'd used before moving up to the murder room—and pulled it out now. There was a small space beside the sofa in the living room that was large enough to fit the mattress and not impede Dimitri's work space, which would do for a few days until I either got over my fear of Edgar's specter or found a better sleeping solution.

With the air-pump roaring, I almost missed the knock at the door. I scrambled up and opened the original Victorian front door, which towered at eight feet and had an intricate side lights and a stained-glass transom crowning its top.

"Ryan," I said. "What a surprise."

"Thought I'd check on you after what happened yesterday." His soothing Scottish accent made me smile, despite the context. Ryan, the town's pharmacist, was almost as new to Starry Cove as I was, having moved here a few months before me. It was Arthur's pharmacy he took over after Arthur passed away, and he and I had grown close over our joint newness in town.

"I guess everyone probably knows by now?"

"Aye. You didn't expect Lovie to pass up the opportunity to gossip about other people, did you? Besides, it was hard to miss the crime scene tape wrapped around the house."

I shook my head. "Just another day in Starry Cove." I led him inside and he got his first look at the current status of Arthur's old mansion.

"Quite an improvement," he said, taking in the chaotic scene.

"I know it's a mess, and Deputy Todd shut down my renovations until this murder gets solved."

His face grew dark. "Are you all right? Truly?"

"I'm fine, really. But I could do with a change of subject. You know now how my project is going, so how is yours?"

"Ah," he said, turning away slightly. "You must mean my gazebo."

"Any progress?"

"If you consider replacing the same part I'd worked on three times now progress, then yes."

When I'd first met Ryan, he shared his desire to build a gazebo at the house he owned in Starry Cove. Small, diminutive, properly dressed in a V-neck sweater and pressed pants, Ryan did not come across as a D-I-Y superhero, and his skills were even less impressive than one could imagine. He'd been reluctant to ask for help from the locals, even Trevor who owned the hardware store, since he feared it would saddle him with a poor reputation among the more blue-collar men in town.

"Well," I said, "I know of a carpenter who's probably

out of work right now. He's just an apprentice level, but he mentioned he'd worked on all types of projects—decks, houses, that sort of thing."

Ryan cocked his head, doubtful. "And is this individual, ah, discreet?"

"I'm sure he can be, but I think you're silly for not wanting help."

"Aye, probably. But a man's ego is not something to toy with so flippantly."

"You have a doctorate degree. What on earth do you need to prove?"

Ryan held a hand up to my face. "My hands are as soft as a baby's bottom, Poppy. Don't you know a man's true worth is based on the number of calluses his calluses have?"

I grabbed his hand and stroked it softly. "Maybe to one another, but not to me. Don't you think it would be nice to enjoy some time in the gazebo? We could have dinner…"

He considered me suspiciously as I caressed his hand. The gears were turning.

"You beguile me," he said after a moment. "I have the sudden urge to ask you to dinner tonight."

"Too bad your gazebo isn't finished," I said, dismissing the notion.

"I meant at Shelby's Diner. Are you free?"

I had every intention of accepting but pretended to play it cool. "I suppose I'm free for Shelby's."

"Excellent," he said. "So, what do you plan to do in the meantime while your construction is on hold?"

"I have no idea, but Deputy Todd seems to think the chief suspect is Blister, my general contractor—and

Angie's cousin—so there're a few wrenches in my plans already."

"Perhaps you could take the time to visit your sister," he said. "I know you had mentioned it before."

I'm sure he chose his words carefully, knowing my sister and I were on touchy ground. We'd had a bit of a reconciliation recently, but our relationship would never be close. "Lily's splitting her time between Baltimore, where she's trying that experimental cancer treatment, and New York. She's collaborating with some actress on a new hat collection. I don't think she wants to slow down, even if it's for her own good."

"The treatments aren't helping?" he asked.

"She says they are, but I can hear it in her voice. She sounds tired. We don't talk very often."

"Well, let's hope things turn out for the better." He stepped toward the front door. "I've got to get back to the pharmacy, but I'll see you tonight. Seven o'clock?"

"Sure, see you then."

***

I continued to set up my makeshift bedroom in the living room space not being co-opted for the renovation team's workspace. I finished blowing up the air mattress, and I'd moved over a little crate to serve as a nightstand. The sofa was still accessible for guests. As I sat there, looking at the mess before me, tatty sofa the only seating available in this expansive mansion, I closed my eyes and cried—just a little—at the absurdity of it all. It was difficult to imagine one day when this place would be a bustling hub of activity. I'd imagined there'd be book club meetings, birthday parties, weddings, and other special events booked solid, enough to keep me busy year-round. But now, I was back to a dingy little living space, all sense of progress lost.

"Poppy?" came a voice at the door.

"It's open, Harper. Come in."

Harper stepped into the living room area and saw my little encampment. "Back here, eh?"

"I couldn't stomach the room upstairs."

"I don't blame you. Here, I brought coffee."

"Thanks." I took the cup from her, thankful that my friend knew exactly how to raise my spirits.

Mayor Dewey appeared and jumped onto the arm of the sofa—a spot he'd claimed as his own over the course of my time in Starry Cove.

"He followed me in. He's been spending a lot of time here, lately." She reached down and scratched him behind the ears. "Haven't you, fuzzy mister mayor man?" Dewey raised up to meet her hand and purred like a little engine.

"Ryan just came by," I said.

"Oh yeah? You two make any plans?"

"Dinner tonight."

"Don't tell me you're going to Shelby's Diner—"

Heavy pounding on the front door stopped Harper with her mouth open.

"Who could that be?" The urgency of the knocking concerned me.

More pounding.

"I'm coming," I shouted as Harper and I rushed to the door.

I opened it to find a tiny woman, all scraggly gray hair and wrinkled skin, staring up at me from the porch with clear blue eyes. How this little thing managed to pound the door so hard she nearly beat it down I don't know, but there she stood.

"Can I help you?" I asked.

"Who are you?" she replied, peering behind us into the house. "I'm looking for Arthur Lewis."

"Oh. I'm so sorry, but Arthur Lewis died a few months ago. I'm his niece, Poppy. I inherited the house. Did you know him?"

The woman's face dropped at the news. Her wrinkles sagged and her blue eyes lost their sparkle. "I did know him."

"Would you like to come in? I didn't catch your name."

"You can call me Greta," she said, stepping into the house.

"I'm sorry." I kicked a bit of discarded wood out of the way. "The house is being renovated, so it's a mess at the moment."

She looked around, taking in all the plastic sheeting and sawdust. "You're tearing it all up."

"Well, I'm renovating it. It will still have its old charm when the construction is finished. There'll be wall paper—"

"You're ripping away Arthur's home," she howled, looking around at the destruction.

"Hey," Harper piped in. "This is Poppy's home now, lady. How did you say you knew Arthur? Because I've lived in this town my entire life and I've never seen you before."

"I didn't say. Arthur and I were colleagues on a project."

"What kind of project?" I asked.

"Oh, this and that. Nothing you'd understand."

"Sounds very scientific," Harper quipped, losing her patience for the little woman.

I hadn't quite had my fill of rudeness yet—news of Arthur's death probably came as a shock to her. "Something pharmaceutical?"

"No, no. Nothing like that. Arthur and I shared many interests—hobbies, you might call them."

Mayor Dewey wandered over and wedged his plump ginger body between Harper's legs.

"I see that fat cat is still here," said Greta. "Dewey, was it?"

Harper and I exchanged a quick glance.

"You know him?" Harper asked.

"Didn't you hear me, young lady?" Her long gray hair waved as shook her head in disappointment. "I said, Arthur and I worked together and that cat was always trying to crawl into my lap. He was barely a kitten back then. Annoying little fellow when you're trying to get anything done."

I guess this woman did know Arthur—probably better than I did. I barely knew my uncle when I found out he'd left his entire estate to me in his will. It was quite a shock, to say the least.

"I'm very sorry you had to find out about Arthur's death this way," I said. "Is there anything I can do for you?"

"Actually," she responded, tapping her fingers together. "Did he happen to leave you a notebook?"

Four

I DON'T THINK Harper or I masked our surprise very well, since Greta smiled and nodded at our reaction to her question. "So, you do have the notebook."

"What are you talking about?" asked Harper. "What's your interest in anything of Arthur's?"

Greta just nodded again, then toddled to the sofa and sat down with a heavy sigh. Her clothes seemed to be about the same age as the sofa, worn and threadbare. Mayor Dewey strolled over and hopped into her lap. He turned around a few times before settling in for a nap.

"I have not seen Arthur for at least, oh, going on ten years now. We'd been working on a project together—"

Harper interrupted, "Yes, you've already said that."

Greta pursed her lips. "You're an impatient one, aren't you?"

I held a hand up to Harper to settle her down then turned back to Greta. "Please, go on."

"First, swear to me the notebook is safe."

"I swear it." I'd stowed that specific inheritance

securely in a safe deposit box in the nearby town of Vista, though I left that part out, still unsure if I could trust this woman.

This appeared to be sufficient, as she continued, "Good, good. Arthur and I had learned of a… a *mystery* surrounding these parts."

"Mystery?"

"That's right. Do you know what was in that notebook?"

"Bunch of scribbles," said Harper.

"Oh, those weren't scribbles, I assure you. They're the answer—or as close to an answer as anyone's gotten—to solving the mystery."

This was all a little too esoteric for me. "Arthur was a pharmacist."

"Yes," she said, leaning in, "and I'm sure he had absolutely no secrets and you've found absolutely nothing that left you wondering what type of man he truly was."

She had me there. Arthur left many things that made me question what he'd been up to. There was the Victorian furniture for one, the secret room in the basement, the antique weaponry—I could go on, but Greta was right, and the look on her face told me she knew it.

"Okay, but why now?" I asked. "You said you and Arthur hadn't spoken for over ten years. What brings you here now?"

"You said the notebook is safe, yes?"

I nodded.

She rustled in a pocket in her long skirt and pulled out a dingy scrap of paper, no larger than a matchbook.

"Have you ever seen this symbol?"

We studied the symbol scrawled on the paper fragment, but it didn't ring any bells with me, and Harper, too, shook her head after a moment.

Greta's face darkened. "There are forces working against me—against what Arthur stood for and what he sought."

"What is it?" I asked.

Harper looked at Greta doubtfully. "This is getting a little weird."

"This is the symbol of a group known as the Gold Hand. They must never get that notebook. Their greed and disregard for the rich history of this area would cause more harm that you can imagine."

"I told you the notebook is safe."

"You must give it to me," Greta urged, grabbing my sleeve. "I must find out what it is and what it all means. Arthur would have wanted me to have it."

"Whoa there, lady." Harper stood up and pried Greta's hands off me. "If Arthur wanted you to have the notebook, why didn't he leave it to you? I think you've said enough—whatever your scam is—and now it's time to go."

My hackles had risen too, and I was wary about this

woman's intent. The pained and burning look in her eyes when she'd grabbed me left me cold.

Greta stood, dumping Dewey onto the floor. "Arthur *would* have left it to me, but he thought I was dead long ago."

"Whatever your story is, the notebook is safe," I repeated. "That's all you need to know. And now I think you should leave."

Greta's eyes shifted from Harper to me, sizing up her chances—to do what, I wasn't sure, but she realized whatever she was after wasn't going to happen. Not today.

"I'm sorry," she said, wild eyes returning to normal. "You must understand my urgency in the matter."

"Uh, yeah, we got it," said Harper, holding out her arm to lead the tiny woman into the foyer and out the door.

On the threshold, Greta stopped and turned back to us. "They'll be looking for it," she whispered. "There are spies in your midst. I'll pray for your safety."

Harper shut the door behind her, a little more forcefully than necessary, and we watched as she skittered down the walkway and out of sight. "What cave did she crawl out of? What a piece of work."

"You were pretty mean," I said, still pondering what Greta had said.

"And she was pretty crazy. And clearly trying to scam you out of whatever that notebook is. I'm wondering if Angie was right and it's some famous artist's sketchbook or something—worth real money."

"But she said people were after it. And they have been, remember?" It wasn't too long ago we'd had some close shaves associated with that book, which was the reason I'd secured it in Vista in the first place.

Harper considered this. "I guess you're right, but this lady..."

"And she knew Dewey."

"Yeah, I guess so. Hey, you don't think she and Arthur were—you know?"

"What?" I asked, incredulous. "No way. Well, I mean, maybe. I wouldn't put it past Arthur to keep surprising us from the grave."

"What did you think of that symbol thing?"

"Hmm, I don't know."

"I didn't want to say anything, but I think I've seen it somewhere—or it felt like I have—but I can't place it."

"Why didn't you say something before?" I asked.

Harper shook her head. "I don't trust that lady. I'm not sharing anything with her. But I'm sure I've seen it somewhere."

Five

DESPITE HOW STRANGE the day had already been, I was still no closer to having my crew back and renovations moving, and I could best spend my time figuring out how to clear Blister's name. He'd mentioned that Maisie was Edgar's ex-wife, and Harper and Angie and I felt like she'd probably have some information that may help—if she wasn't the culprit herself.

Harper had already left to finish her mail rounds, and I shook off Greta's words as best I could as I threw my bag into my Prius and hit the road to Vista. On the way out of town I spotted Mayor Jim, a fresh stack of flyers in hand, talking with a couple at the roundabout. *Always schmoozing, that one.*

Vista was a larger town up the road from Starry Cove to the north, although not on the coast. It contained many of the larger shops and county buildings and was a frequent destination for many of Starry Cove's residents.

Angie had shared directions to the new shopping center under construction—Vista was still new to me—

and I parked along the side of the street next to a chain link privacy fence erected around the property. I could hear construction going on from the other side—the telltale whizzes and bangs of hand tools and hammers—but opaque plastic sheeting covered the fence and obscured my view into the job site.

"Can I help you?" a man's gruff voice called from behind me.

I turned to find an enormous hairy man, arms crossed, eyes flattened, staring down at me in disapproval. "Sorry, I know how this looks. I'm here looking for a plumber named Maisie. I was told she might be working on this new shopping center. Do you know her?"

His face did not change. "This is a construction site, lady. You'll need to leave. And your car is parked in a no-parking zone." He nodded behind him, where my Prius waited against the fence between two safety cones.

"Oh, sorry. So, you don't know Maisie?"

"I don't talk about who is or isn't on my crew. Now beat it."

Well, that first approach didn't work out too well, but I wasn't giving up. I hopped back into my car and drove around to the back of the site, off the main road. Maybe there was a box or something I could stand on to see over the fence.

I parked the car behind a dumpster and crept up to the fence line. There was a trash can filled with rocks or something heavy and placed on one of the fence footers for stability and I climbed on top to peer over. There was no one around this part of the site that I could tell, but as luck would have it, a moment later Maisie's tiny frame strode into sight carrying her toolbox. She wore her strawberry blonde hair in a long braid today, tucked under a ball cap, but I was sure it was her.

"Psst, Maisie," I whisper-shouted. "Maisie."

She slowed and turned my way. It took her a moment to spot my head poking over the top of the fence and she walked over with a curious look on her face.

"What are you doing?" She peered up at me looming above. She was already very short. and I was standing on the trashcan leaning over a tall fence, probably topping out at eight feet. I must have been an odd sight.

"Your foreman wouldn't let me in to talk to you."

"About what?" Her words were curt.

"I wanted to say I'm sorry about your ex-husband."

She grunted. "Oh yeah? You came all this way and trespassed onto private property tell me that?"

"Okay, well, more than that," I admitted. "Look, the deputy in my town thinks Blister could have done this, but you and I both know he wouldn't have hurt anyone."

"You think you know Blister?"

"I know I don't know any of you very well, but can you think of anyone who would want to hurt Edgar?"

A smile slipped out at the corner of her mouth. "Sure, the whole construction industry. Edgar was a jerk and he drank too much. That's why I divorced him."

"But he loved his kids, right?"

Maisie's eyes narrowed at the mention of her kids. "What do they have to do with anything?"

"Edgar wanted to spend more time with them, right?"

"Where'd you hear that?"

"Blister told me."

"Yeah, well did Blister tell you that Edgar hadn't

paid his child support for the past two months? He had the money to do it, too. I should know—my attorney requested his records for the last hearing. And if there is anything Edgar was good at it was keeping records—guess he liked to know how much money he had to spend on beer."

Clearly, these two weren't on the path to reconciliation. "You don't seem too torn up about his murder."

"And why should I be?" Maisie spat her words and crossed her arms. "Maybe for my kids, but otherwise, good riddance. But I didn't kill him if that's what you're thinking. I'm working three contracts now and I can barely make ends meet." She glanced back toward the worksite. "I've got to go."

I could tell I was working my last thread with her. "Wait," I called as she walked away. "If you can't think of anyone specific who might've had it out for him, can you at least tell me if you saw anything strange at the house that day?"

"Other than your ancient plumbing? Look, I remember seeing Cho and the twins at some point, but no one else. I had my head under your counter most of the day, so all I saw was rust and water damage."

"You didn't see the others?" I asked.

"No, but you'll probably want to talk to Dimitri. He and Edgar were drinking buddies—or were. Dimitri came to me the other day accusing Edgar of stealing money from him. He said it was a good thing I left him, and boy, was he was right."

"Do you know where I can find Dimitri?"

"If he's not working on a site, you can find him at the

bar. They used to go to the Vista Tavern together so they could waste their money getting plastered instead of caring for their kids."

A voice called from somewhere in the maze of construction behind Maisie—the foreman.

"Time for me to go," she said

"Thanks for talking to me Maisie. I really appreciate it. I just want to clear Blister's name."

She walked away but turned back to me as I climbed down the trashcan. "Hey, if you see Dustin and Justin tell them I want my money."

"What's that about?"

"They owe me a hundred dollars from last week's fantasy results, and I could really use that payout right now."

"I will. Thanks again Maisie." I steadied myself on the fence while climbing down off the trashcan and finally set my two feet on the ground.

"Hello, Miss Lewis," came Deputy Todd's voice nearby.

Curses. Deputy Todd managed to sneak up behind me. He must have added rubber soles to his boots because I'd heard nothing. *He's getting stealthier.*

I tried to play it cool, but he'd caught me red-handed. "Hello there, Deputy Todd. What brings you here?"

"I received a report of a trespasser on this property, so I could ask you the same thing." He latched his thumbs in the belt loops of his uniform and stood, lanky and proud, between me and the dumpster where my car sat conspicuous and alone. He had that unreadable look on his face that he did so well that meant he wouldn't believe a word I said. "Imagine my surprise when I drive up and see you teetering on this security fence the very day after I directed you to stay out of this investigation."

I held up my hands in protest. "I was just giving Maisie my condolences. Edgar was her ex-husband, you know."

"Were you now?" he said, unconvinced.

"And I was just leaving," I said, stepping around him toward my car.

"Miss Lewis," Deputy Todd called out after I had passed. "I don't want to run into you like this again, understand?"

"Got it." I quickened my pace and skirted around the dumpster to reach my car, climbing in as quickly as I could. He watched me as I drove off, eyes following my vehicle through the parking lot and out onto the street.

***

My visit to Vista wasn't just to talk to Maisie. The events of the morning had altered my plans to include an additional stop—the bank. Greta's description of the notebook was spot-on, and she knew too much about its contents for it to be a fluke. But I needed to see for myself.

After a brief wait, a bank employee ushered me into the secure room to view the contents of my safe deposit box. It held just one item—the notebook—and I lifted it gingerly out of the steel box and placed it on the table in the middle of the room. The security guard had left, so it was just me alone staring at the notebook, its pages loosely falling out, bits and scraps of paper poked out like multi-colored bookmarks.

I flipped through, careful not to disturb or damage the pages. My eye scanned for any mention of Greta, but

I found nothing that would indicate she had anything to do with it. To be fair, I found no mention of Arthur either, just the same scribbles and odd notations Harper and Angie and I had seen when we'd first found the book hidden in the Victorian mansion.

I planned to leave the book here in the safety of the bank rather than risk taking it back to the house. It still made no sense to me—there was no distinction in any of the sketches, everything was so vague. No names I recognized, no dates—just a big scribbly mystery. Greta had said it had something to do with the area, but I couldn't make heads or tails of it.

But as I closed the notebook, I spotted something on the very last page—a symbol. It was the symbol Greta had shown us for the Gold Hand, but nothing more, sketched in the center of the sheet. The words *"honore inter fures"* then the loose translation of "Honor Amongst Thieves" written underneath.

I needed more heads together to figure this out. Harper and Angie could help, but I didn't want to take the book out of the bank. Instead, I pulled out my phone and took a picture of every single page of that notebook, crisp and clear, to refer to later.

Stowed safely away, I returned the book and box to its spot along the wall and left the bank with few answers and more questions. Greta clearly knew what she was talking about, but whether she was friend or foe, I hadn't decided yet.

***

Maisie's comments from that morning added to my itinerary, and I cruised to a stop in a parking spot outside the Vista Tavern. The parking lot was gravel, not even paved and sounds from the nearby freeway hummed in my ears. The building stood alone in the middle of the gravel desert—just a few beat-up cars and trucks parked outside. I spotted a smattering of businesses across the street, but they were a good way off, giving the bar a wide berth. This was definitely a rougher spot in town.

The Vista Tavern's illuminated sign flickered, and a small piece of the glass in one corner had broken off and lay shattered below. There were no windows in the front of the single-story brick bar. As I headed inside, I realized I hadn't told anyone where I was going. If Dimitri frequented this kind of place and he was the murderer, he and his dodgy bar cronies could very well dispose of me without anyone knowing.

Late afternoon light from the opened front door filled the darkened bar. Ribbons of smoke lit up and drifted through the air before disappearing as the door closed behind me. There were two guys anchored at the bar, staring at a tiny television mounted above the bottles of whiskey lining the far wall. The bartender eyed me dubiously while wiping down a pint glass.

"Hello," I said, approaching the men. "I'm looking for someone named Dimitri."

No response.

"I don't know his last name," I continued, "but he has a heavy Slavic accent. He does drywall."

The two men at the bar sized me up with their eyes but offered no response and turned back to the television.

"You going to order something?" asked the bartender.

I guess no one knew Dimitri, or else they weren't

sharing. "Um, I'll have a beer," I said, sidling up to one barstool.

"A beer," the bartender repeated, his eyes flat. "Coming right up."

"What are you guys watching?" I asked the men at the end of the bar.

Both turned and looked me as if I were a talking horse. They wore matching baseball caps over their greasy hair, which poked out in all directions from underneath.

"Baseball," one of them said.

"Okay. Who's winning?" I asked, hoping to warm them up to me with a little engagement.

"Dodgers," said the other with no emotion.

I couldn't tell from their faces if the Dodgers winning was a good or a bad thing. I glanced at the decorative letter adorning the front of their ball caps. No D in sight, so I took a chance. "Bummer."

The man closest to me eyed me up and down again. "Yeah. They're rotten."

The other man spit on the floor. "Rotten."

"Rotten," I repeated, shaking my head in feigned disgust.

"Here you go," said the bartender, arriving with my beer. It was lukewarm and a faint smear of fingerprints tarnished the glass.

"Thanks," I said. "I guess I'll wait here for Dimitri then."

"You'll be waiting a long time," said the man farthest from me down the bar.

"Really?"

"Yeah. He only comes 'round here about lunchtime.

He likes the food."

"Really?" I asked again, looking around at the dingy bar. The disbelief in my voice made the word squeak out.

"We've got great sandwiches," said the bartender, offended.

"Sorry," I apologized. "I'm sure you do. Was he in here earlier today?"

"Sure was," said the first man. "Kept to himself, though. He's usually up at the bar watching the game with us and sometimes he comes in with another fella, but not today."

"What was your name, miss?" the farthest man asked.

"I'm Poppy. I'm from over in Starry Cove."

"Nice to meet you Poppy. Always good to have another Dodger hater joining in. I'm Hank and this is Gus."

"And you can call me Joe," said the bartender.

"Glad to meet you guys. Too bad I missed Dimitri."

"What'd you want him for, anyway?" asked Gus.

"He's working on a project for me, but I guess I'll catch him here another time." I got up from my seat and left some cash on the bar for the beer. "Plus," I said, giving Joe a wide grin, "I've got to check out the sandwiches sometime."

"Bye Poppy," said Hank. "Come back and cheer against the Dodgers any time."

I left the bar and headed back out into the low sunlight of late afternoon, which still made me squint after being inside that dungeon, even for just a few minutes. The place didn't seem so scary once you got to know the people inside—and I could probably learn to really dislike the Dodgers if I needed to—but dinner with Ryan was at seven, and I still had to get back to Starry Cove and get ready. I'd just have to return to the bar another time to get Dimitri's side of the story.

***

I spiffed myself up by changing out of my fence-straddling, Dodger-hating clothes and into something nicer and headed to the diner down the street from the house.

"Hi Shelby," I said, greeting the owner as I walked in. Shelby stood behind the countertop reorganizing the pies in the case. Her wide body swayed as she hummed a tune and her silver beehive hair flopped to the beat. Shelby's Diner was next to Angie's bakery, so there was always pie to go around in this town. The diner was exactly what one would expect from a small-town diner—good food, nice people, and lots and lots of gossip.

"Poppy," said Shelby, straightening. She seemed surprised to see me. "How are you doing, dearie? Lovie told me everything about yesterday and it's just awful."

"I'm fine, Shelby. Nothing your food can't fix, at least."

"Aren't you precious," she said, blushing. "Are you here for some takeout?"

"No, I'm meeting Ryan." I took a seat at the counter. "We're going to eat here."

"You two are such a cute couple."

"We're not a couple. We're just friends."

"Okay, whatever you say, dearie." She winked. "But you smell awfully nice for 'just friends.'"

"I just showered. I had a messy day."

Shelby automatically filled a coffee mug for me. "Some lady came by asking about your house today," she said. "Wanted to know about Arthur, too. Asked all sorts of questions about that old mansion."

"Really?" My mind immediately thought of Greta, that snoop. She must be sniffing out anything she can about the house and what I've been up to.

Shelby motioned to the front window. "Here comes the doctor now."

Ryan stood on the sidewalk on the other side of Main Street. The tiny town pharmacy was located inside the general store, which was a hop-skip across the street from the diner. He looked both ways before crossing and chimed through the door into the restaurant.

"Hello ladies," he said, greeting us both in his adorable Scottish accent. "Hope I'm not late."

"I just got here. Let's grab our booth." Shelby eyed me slyly as we left the counter and headed to the booth we usually sat at for dinner. *Yeesh, just because we had a special booth didn't mean we were a couple.*

"How are you doing?" he asked as we sat down. "I felt bad leaving you alone this morning."

"I'm fine. Harper came by and then I went up to Vista to run some errands. Anything exciting happen at the pharmacy today?"

"Ursula received a stock of hairbrushes and combs, so that was probably my highlight." Ursula ran the general store, and I depended on Ryan to update me when any new products came in. Last week, she got in a shipment of new cat treats, so I had to pop in and get some for Mayor Dewey. He threw them up on the porch, but it was worth a try.

"Hairbrushes, how riveting."

"I'm sure your day was more exciting than mine. How was Vista?"

"The same as it always is." Sharing my trespassing episode, secret society research, and dodgy bar excursion was not on the menu for tonight, so I kept it simple.

Shelby glided over in her squeaky work clogs. "What'll you have tonight?"

"I'll have more coffee and the grilled cheese," I said.

"Excellent choice," Ryan said, nodding his head while reading the menu. "I think I'll have the—"

"Burger and fries, Doctor?" Shelby said before he could finish.

"Actually, I'm going to try something different."

"You are?" Shelby and I asked together. Ryan always ordered the burger and fries—this was new ground.

"Aye. I'm going to have the *cheeseburger* this time. With *chips* please."

Shelby gave him an exasperated look and stared down as though she might say something before shutting her mouth, closing her order pad, and heading back into the kitchen.

"Not very different," I said. "And she didn't correct your 'chips' to 'fries' like she usually does."

He shrugged. "I guess the joke's getting old." Ryan and Shelby had an ongoing tussle over the correct word to use for what Americans call French fries. "Anyway, I took your advice and contacted that Quentin fellow who does construction. He'll be out at the house tomorrow. I guess the only project he had going was your house."

"He's an apprentice carpenter, remember? I think he has to work on real projects with his carpenter master—who's now deceased."

"Aye. Sorry to bring up Edgar again, but I don't think there'll be an issue with Quentin working on a small outdoor project like my gazebo. Couldn't be much worse than what I've done to it already."

I chuckled. "Yeah, probably not." Ryan's deftness at the carpentry arts was non-existent. "Would you mind if I stopped by the house tomorrow? I wanted to talk to Quentin and now I know where he'll be."

"No, go ahead."

A few minutes later Shelby arrived with our orders. My grilled cheese was perfect—hot and gooey, but when she placed Ryan's plate in front of him, there was nothing on it except a lone cheeseburger.

"Where's my chips?" he lamented, looking up at her with his puppy dog eyes.

Shelby smirked and pulled a small crinkled plastic bag of potato chips from her apron and dropped them on the table. "Your *chips*, Doctor. Enjoy."

I couldn't help but grin as she walked away. "Shelby one, Ryan zero. You've got to admit, she got you there."

"I suppose so," he said. "I don't even like potato crisps."

"*Crisps?*" I shook my head.

Six

THE FOLLOWING DAY I woke early, probably because I was sleeping on an air mattress in the middle of a war zone. I chugged a cup of coffee and headed straight to the bakery to meet up with Angie. Harper would probably follow soon after—she wasn't a morning person, and a stop and Angie's bakery for coffee and a cinnamon roll had become her normal routine.

"Morning Poppy," Angie greeted me as I walked in.

"Smells great in here. What are you making?"

"I've had a special order in for my apple huckleberry pie, so I've been baking my tushy off all morning."

"Got any cinnamon rolls left?"

"Of course. I saved two just for you and Harper." Angie rustled with something on the back counter before producing a fresh cinnamon roll on a plate.

Harper slumped through the door. "Coffee. Pronto. And you've got to polish your Pie Parade trophy, Angie. I can't see it gleaming from fifty yards away anymore."

"Here you go." Angie handed Harper a steaming cup

of coffee and a cinnamon roll.

"You're the best." Harper took a seat with me at the small table against the wall. "How was the date last night?"

"You had a date last night?" asked Angie, toddling over with her own coffee and plate of goodies.

"Ryan and I had dinner. It wasn't a date."

"You keep saying these dates aren't dates. I don't think you know what a date is, Poppy."

"I do. Don't be silly. Anyway, Shelby mentioned Greta."

Harper sat up straight. "That crazy lady?"

"What crazy lady?" Angie asked, sitting down with us to eat her own cinnamon roll. She looked from Harper to me then back to Harper again.

"Some old lady came by Poppy's house yesterday demanding we hand over the notebook to her."

"The notebook?" Angie asked, surprised. "How'd she know about that?"

"She said she was an old colleague of Arthur's, but we made her leave. I checked out the book again while I was in Vista yesterday."

"Do you have it with you?"

"No, I took pictures of all the pages instead. I didn't want to take it out of the safe deposit box."

"Gosh, that was smart," said Angie. "What did you find out?"

"Greta claimed there was some secret group looking for the notebook and that it had clues to some mystery about this area. Harper, that symbol Greta showed us? It was in the notebook."

"What symbol?" Angie asked through the crumbs

tumbling out of her mouth. "I can't believe I missed all this excitement."

I pulled a pencil from my bag and quickly sketched it onto a napkin for Angie. "Maybe that's where you remembered seeing it, Harper. In the notebook itself."

"Maybe, but it doesn't seem quite right."

"Well, besides checking out the notebook I managed to talk to Maisie, too. It was no easy feat and Deputy Todd is pretty peeved at me, but she shared some interesting information."

"Did she seem like the killer?" Harper asked. "Ex-spouses are always the guilty party."

"I'm not so sure. For one, Maisie is really short—how would she shoot a nail gun straight into Edgar's head?"

"Oh, Poppy, don't be so gruesome. I'm trying to eat here," said Angie.

"Sorry. Anyway, Maisie also needed Edgar's child support. Although she did mention he hadn't paid in a few months…"

"Well there you go," said Harper. "She was mad that Edgar hadn't paid up."

"She also mentioned that Dimitri accused Edgar of stealing money from him."

Angie finished chewing her last bite. "You should talk to Dimitri, then. That sounds like a motive too."

I shook my head. "I already tried. I went to the Vista Tavern looking for him."

"Whoa. That place is rough."

"The bartender and the guys there were actually pretty nice. I'll go back in a few days when I know he'll be there."

But Harper was only half listening and instead glared at something through the front window. I turned to follow her stare. Mayor Jim walked by with a bag of takeout, probably from Shelby's next door.

"You really don't like that man, do you?"

"I don't know why he gets under my skin so bad. I think anyone could do a better job as mayor. Even Mayor Dewey would make a better mayor than that wet sock."

"He's running unopposed, so you'll just have to accept it," said Angie.

Harper groaned and put her head in her hands, then perked back up. "What if he didn't run unopposed?"

"Yay," Angie said, clapping her hands. "You're going to run?"

"No, not me. What if Mayor Dewey ran for mayor?"

"The cat?" I asked to be sure. "For mayor?"

"Yeah. He's way more popular than Jim. The whole town knows him, and the job is basically showing up for town events, which he already does anyway."

"It's an interesting idea." Angie eyed her sideways, unsure if Harper was serious.

"I don't know, Harper…"

"Seriously. I think I'm on to something here. I just need a little time to work it out."

"There's a town meeting tonight. I assume we're all going?" asked Angie.

"Oh no," I said. "I forgot all about it. It'll be nothing except gawking and gossiping about Edgar's murder."

Angie placed a hand on my arm. "We'll be there with you. And the town knows you now—they're on your side."

"Yeah, and if anyone gets out of line, we'll put them

back in it."

The town meetings were the most exciting thing that happened in Starry Cove, other than the occasional murder. The entire town shows up to mingle and munch on the snacks and treats Shelby and others provide. With recent events at the big mansion, this town meeting was sure to be standing room only.

Angie gathered up our finished plates. "What are you going to do the rest of the day, Poppy, now that the renovations are on hold?"

"I was hoping to talk to Cho, but I don't know where to find her."

"Oh," said Angie. "I saw her go into the diner earlier this morning. She may still be there."

"Cho?" asked Harper. "What about her? What do you need to ask?"

"Blister said she asked about who was going to be on the job, remember? He said when she found out where it was and that Edgar would be a part of the crew, she signed on immediately. Doesn't that sound suspicious?"

"Maybe."

Angie nodded. "Wouldn't hurt to ask her since you weren't able to get any info from Dimitri yesterday. She may have something more to share."

I gathered up my things. "Thanks for breakfast, Angie. I'll see you guys later for the town meeting."

"Wish I could go with you, but I got to go too," said Harper. "Thanks Angie. See you tonight—should be fun."

***

I popped over to the diner next door and spotted Cho

almost immediately. Her slick black hair was back in a ponytail and despite it being a warm morning, she wore a long sleeve work shirt and overalls. She sat at the counter, in a spot that used to be reserved for someone else. I shook off that memory—best not to think about it.

"Hi Cho," I said, taking the seat next to her.

"Hi Poppy. I heard about Edgar." She shook her head in disbelief. "I'm so sorry."

"It's all right. I've got thick skin. Sorry the work's been shut down. Do you have another job lined up?"

"Not yet, but I'm working on it. I was already scheduled off yesterday and I didn't get the message about Edgar and the house until I'd already arrived this morning. I came over here instead to get a bite to eat."

"The food here is great. I recommend the griddle cakes or the swiss cheese omelet."

"I'm glad you said that—I already ordered the omelet."

A skinny teenage server with freckles and spiky red hair walked up and asked if I wanted coffee. Clearly, he didn't know me. "Yes, coffee please. Where's Shelby?"

"She's out today, miss," said the young man, his voice squeaking. "Not sure why."

I'd hoped to catch Shelby again to ask her about the woman who'd come into the diner and asked a bunch of questions about the house. I'd have to remember to catch her another time. He filled my mug then I turned back to Cho. "Are you doing okay? I know you guys knew Edgar pretty well."

Cho scoffed. "I'm fine, trust me."

"I take it Edgar and you weren't the best of friends?"

Cho looked straight at me. "No one liked Edgar. No

one will miss him. You'll find that out by asking anyone he's ever worked with."

"Blister said you asked about who was working on the project. Edgar didn't scare you off?"

"Nothing scares me. I just want to get back to work, okay?" She turned away, staring at the kitchen door, waiting for her food.

"I do too. But until Deputy Todd lifts the stop order, my project is on hold. Can you think of anyone who'd do this to Edgar? Or do you remember anything that might have seemed strange?"

"I don't know," she replied. "Blister had been really short with Edgar lately—probably tired of his attitude. Blister doesn't fly off the handle often, but he sure lost his patience with that man." She turned to face me again. "I do remember something strange that happened recently. I was talking to Quentin a few days ago, and he said he'd soon be the only carpenter working on the job. And now Edgar is out of the picture. How do you think Quentin would have known that?"

"That is strange," I admitted.

"He came up to me alone, like it was some big secret. He sounded excited too, but I guess Quentin's always a bit over-excited. And a bit of a brownnoser too, if you know what I mean."

"Quentin's just the apprentice though, right? How could he be the only carpenter on the project?"

"I think he's close to finishing the apprenticeship—it's been a few years, at least. I don't really keep up with his status though—that was Edgar's job."

"Can you think of anything else that might be helpful?"

"Yeah, don't forget about Edgar's ex-wife—that's Maisie, if you didn't know. I don't know about you, but I wouldn't have wanted to work onsite with my ex-anything. If I hated Edgar, then she must have *loathed* him."

"Right," I said, already onto that lead. "What about Dustin and Justin? Do you know where I could find them?"

Cho shook her head. "No clue. I didn't know those guys very well. They always seemed kind of shady to me."

The squeaky teenager came out of the kitchen with Cho's breakfast.

"I'll let you eat. Thanks for helping me out." I left some change on the counter for the coffee.

"See you later," she said through a mouthful of food as I headed out the door.

Not good news for Blister—Cho had confirmed he and Edgar were on rocky ground before the murder. But at least I had a lead—Quentin had some explaining to do and, lucky for me, I knew exactly where to find him.

Seven

I ARRIVED AT Ryan's bungalow at lunchtime. The one-story house was close to the main part of town on the same road that Angie's house was on. It sat back on the property, secluded, with a porch in the front up a few steps that led to the front door. I wasn't going inside, though, instead I eased open the side gate and walked into the backyard which was good-sized, but still a bit soggy from the recent rains. My shoes squished into the wet ground, shooting excess water to the side with each step. The gazebo—or half a gazebo—sat in the far corner away from the house. A stack of redwood planks waited nearby to be used.

I didn't spot Quentin immediately, instead, he spotted me.

"Poppy, what are you doing here?"

"Hi Quentin. Ryan said you'd be here, so I wanted to come by and take a look at this gazebo he's been telling me about."

He turned off his saw, set it down, and slapped the

sawdust off his pants. "It's not finished yet, but hopefully by the end of the day if the weather holds up. This is a fairly easy construction and shouldn't take a whole lot of time."

"Don't tell Ryan that—it's taken him months just to get this far." We both looked at the structure, off kilter and incomplete.

"I won't. But I also know he wants it done pretty quickly."

I nodded. "I'm sorry about Edgar. You two must have been pretty close."

"We were," said Quentin, walking over to the gazebo. He put a hand on a wobbly rail. "We'd been working together for years, so it was a nasty shock."

"Do you know who would have wanted to do something like this? It seems so violent, like there was a lot of anger in it."

"I've been wondering that since last night when I got the call. It's hard to believe anyone on the crew could be involved."

"I heard that Edgar wasn't exactly everyone's friend."

Quentin glanced at me. "Caught that, did you?" He picked up bits of scrap wood and carried them to a small pile nearby. "Yeah, Edgar was a jerk, to be honest. But he was a jerk to everyone, me included. It was just who he was. Since I worked with him for so long, I learned to let it wash off my back, but I can imagine those who didn't understand would find Edgar to be pretty nasty."

"And were there people on the crew who didn't understand?"

"I think they all disliked Edgar, but murder? No

way."

"Someone mentioned that you said you'd be the only carpenter on the site soon."

His lips pursed. "I knew Cho couldn't keep her mouth shut."

"Did you know something?" I pressed.

Quentin sat down on the base of the gazebo. It tottered a bit, and he put a hand down to steady himself. "I'm close to taking my licensing test. Once I pass, I'll be on my own."

"But what about Edgar? How did you know he wouldn't be on the job anymore?"

"Because he told me he was going to start his own business as a general contractor. Said he'd let others do the hard work from now on. I also think he thought it would impress Maisie."

"Impress Maisie?" I asked. This was interesting. Edgar wanted to start a business to impress her. I doubt it would have worked after having spoken with Maisie—she seemed pretty set in her desire to stay apart.

"Yeah, she's his ex-wife—not sure if you knew that. He never wanted a divorce—it was all her. I was his apprentice through the entire thing. The worst days were coming in to work on a job after they'd had another fight or something about the kids."

"That must have been hard."

"I felt terrible for those kids. They both cared about them, but Maisie wanted to keep Edgar away. He drank a bit, if you didn't know."

"So, you wouldn't have worked with Edgar at his new business? You'd stay on with Blister?"

"Blister's great. Edgar though…" Quentin shook his

head. "He was my carpentry master, but man, he was tough to work with. I've been counting the days until this apprenticeship is over. I'm not sure what I'll do now that he's gone. I'll have to find another carpenter to finish out with."

"That's got to be tough. How far are you away from your exam?"

"About a month and a half."

I whistled. "Really close then. Well, I hope the work on the house will start up again before that, but until this business with Edgar gets sorted out, I'm in the lurch."

"What are you going to do?"

"Wait until it's solved, I guess. Can you remember anything that might be helpful, or do you remember seeing anything out of the ordinary that day?"

Quentin leaned back on the gazebo floor with both arms back. He chewed his lip. "Have you talked to Dustin and Justin yet?"

"Not yet. Should I?"

"Well, Edgar and I had gone onto the back porch to throw some scraps of wood into the waste pile and Edgar, uh, had some vulgar words for those two."

"What did he say?"

"I won't repeat it, but I can tell you Edgar was hot about something, really mad. If those two boys weren't trapped in the mud, I thought Edgar would have gone out and pounded them right then."

"What was the fight about?"

"Fantasy."

"Fantasy?" I asked.

"Yeah, fantasy league stuff. Seems those guys owed a lot of money. They even owe me from my win on

Sunday. If you see them, tell them I want my money."

"I will. Do you remember anything else?"

"Maybe what I *didn't* see. I didn't see Dimitri at all near the end of our work. I remember going out to the living room—that's where he's set up, you remember?"

I nodded. Yes, I remembered. I was currently living in a small patch of that very living room surrounded by Dimitri's half-finished projects.

"I go out into the living room and he wasn't there. And I looked around on the ground floor. He wasn't there." He shrugged. "Maybe he'd left already."

"Maybe."

"Is it true that it was his nail gun?"

"Yeah, but Blister said everyone used it."

"That's true, we all did. It was a nice gun. Powerful, accurate."

"Do you think Dimitri—"

"Hello there, you two," Ryan called as he entered the yard. He trudged over to us stepping on patches of grass trying to avoid the mud. "How's the gazebo going?"

Quentin stood up, wiped his hands on his pants, and shook Ryan's hand. "Going well Dr. MacKenzie. I hope to have it completed by the end of the day. I've got the braces set up and the basic framing sections built out."

Ryan nodded his head a few times. "Sounds great." He had no clue what Quentin was talking about, I knew it. I was just getting into some good questions when he arrived, too, and now it would have to wait.

"I won't keep you from your work, Quentin." I waved goodbye and walked into the front yard with Ryan.

"Do you have any idea what he was jabbering about?" Ryan whispered once we were out of earshot.

"He's working very hard and hopes to finish today. That's all you need to know."

Ryan nodded. "Okay, good."

"Are you going to be at the town meeting tonight?"

"Aye. I planned on it. Why?"

"Nothing. I just want to make sure I have some support. No doubt the topic of Edgar's murder in my house will come up, and no doubt the gossips will be out in force."

"Gotcha. Don't worry. I've got your back."

"Thanks Ryan," I said, heading to my car. "I'll see you there."

Eight

"Hurry, it's going to start any minute." Angie ushered us into the community center meeting hall. "I want to get a good seat."

Harper peeled off. "I'm going to hit the snack bar first. Shelby made miniature cheesecakes. What'd you bring, Angie?"

"Roy brought some donut holes from the bakery."

"Donut holes? That's pretty weak for the town meeting."

Angie frowned. "We've been really busy, okay?"

"All right, all right," said Harper. "Don't get angry—you turn red and puff up like a little bulldog."

"C'mon Angie," I said. "Let's get seats over here." I led her away from Harper to an empty row of chairs near the back of the room by the double entry doors. It would get stuffy inside once it was crammed with people, and I wanted to sit near some fresh air and an easy escape.

Angie pointed toward the door. "There's Dewey."

Mayor Dewey glided in and rubbed up against

Shelby's leg as she stood near the door. She leaned down and gave him a gentle pet before he moved on to the next person and did it all over again. Rub, pet. Rub, pet. Once he reached the end of our row, he jumped up onto the chairs and walked over, his ginger belly swaying.

"Hey buddy," I said. "Come to catch the spectacle?"

"The snacks, more likely."

Dewey meowed at us before hopping down and disappearing under the row of chairs in front of us.

Harper shuffled into the seat we'd saved for her, arms full of snacks—enough to last her the whole meeting.

"I saw Dewey come in," she said. "Handsome little guy, huh?"

"You aren't still thinking of having him run for mayor, are you?" asked Angie.

"Why not? He's more qualified than Jim—the people actually like him."

Angie turned to me. "What do you think, Poppy? Would you vote for Dewey over Jim?"

I shrugged. "Probably."

"Gosh. I hate to admit it, but me too."

"We'd have to add a litter box to town hall though," I said. We all glanced toward the door at the side of the room that led to what Angie called the tiniest town hall in the county. It was a single room no larger than ten feet by eight at most, with a single desk, currently occupied by Mayor Jim during the day.

"Worth it," said Harper.

"Did you find out anything new today, Poppy?"

"I talked to Cho and Quentin, the apprentice. Cho was pretty straight with me—said everyone hated Edgar. She also told me that Quentin mentioned to her a few days ago that he'd be the only carpenter soon."

"Whoa," Harper sputtered, choking on her miniature cheesecake before recovering. "Like, he knew Edgar would be dead?"

"That's what it sounded like from Cho's end, but when I talked to Quentin, turns out Edgar was going to start his own general contracting business—that's where he'd be going, leaving Quentin alone on the house project."

"Did Cho seem suspicious at all?" asked Angie.

"She didn't seem to hide anything, but she wasn't exactly forthcoming. She wants to get back to work, at least, so I know she wants the murder solved."

"I wouldn't believe it was Cho over the other crew members," said Harper. "She wasn't like the rest of them."

"What about Blister?" asked Angie. "He's not guilty either. Why are you so dismissive of Cho? We don't know her at all."

"I'm just saying she wasn't like the others there. She was laid back—seemed like a cool chick, that's all."

"After hearing what Quentin had to say about Edgar, I'm inclined to think Cho just misunderstood what he meant. But Cho also mentioned Maisie as a suspect—no surprise, being his ex-wife—and she also mentioned that Blister and Edgar had been fighting recently. Not fighting-fighting, but, um, exchanging heated words."

Angie looked from me to Harper, eyes wide. "You two don't think Blister could be guilty, do you?"

I put my arm around her and gave her a gentle squeeze. "Of course not. It just makes it more important that we find out who really killed Edgar."

"What else did Quentin say?" Harper asked, shoving a cookie into her mouth. "He worked close with Edgar, right?" A few crumbs dribbled out and onto the floor.

"Apparently Edgar called out Dustin and Justin—the two laborers who were out in the rain—over some fantasy sports thing. He wasn't the first to mention that those two owed money to a lot of people."

"Where are they now? With your house renovations shut down, they could be working anywhere."

"Yeah, and no one seems to know where I can find them—only that they want me to remind them they owe money once I do."

"Money is a nasty temptress," said Harper. "We know that."

Angie shook her head. "I'd hate to think people could murder over something so trivial, but it's definitely possible."

"Probable," I corrected. "There seems to be a lot of money issues going around."

"What are you going to do next?" asked Angie.

"I'm going to try finding Dimitri again. Quentin said Dimitri disappeared right before Blister called off the work that day. I've got quite a few questions for him."

"Looks like the meeting's starting." Harper tossed another cookie in her mouth. "Settle in."

Ryan caught my eye from the corner and gave me a thumbs up as Mayor Jim stepped up to the podium. I smiled back, thankful for the support.

The mayor cleared his throat and the feedback from the microphone filled the room. Everyone in attendance covered their ears.

"Sorry, sorry," he said, stepping back. "Is that better?

Good. I want to welcome everyone—it appears we have quite a large crowd tonight, so I'll get right to it. Now, it is with a sad and heavy heart that I announce the passing of Edgar Biggs, a resident of Vista who tragically died while working on the renovations at the Lewis mansion."

All eyes shifted my way, boring into my soul. Angie squeezed my hand.

"Deputy Todd Newman has asked to say a few words to our community about recent events. Deputy, come on up." Mayor Jim motioned for Deputy Todd to step up to the podium.

The deputy placed a small notecard on the dais and scanned the audience. His eyes stopped on me, then moved on to finish scanning the room. A hint of a grimace flashed across his face when he spied Veronica Valentine, reporter for the *Vista View* newspaper, clutching her voice recorder at the ready.

"As Mayor Jim reported, there was a death two days ago at the Lewis residence on Main Street. The Sheriff's Office—that's me—is currently investigating this act as a homicide. I recommend all residents take precaution for their own safety. Lock your doors, windows, and only go out in groups. Don't answer your door unless it's someone you know personally. If you—"

Veronica stood up in the front row, her blonde bob cut a severe line across her face and her red glasses curled at the tips like tiny horns working their way out of her head. "Deputy, if I may?" began Veronica. "You said—"

"You may not, Miss Valentine," shot Deputy Todd. "I'll tell you when I'm done speaking and then you can ask your questions."

Veronica sat down quietly and whispered something

into the small recorder.

"As I was saying, if anyone observes anything suspicious, you are asked to contact the Sheriff's Office—that's me—immediately. Thank you. I'll now take any—"

"Deputy Todd," Veronica said, shooting up out of her chair. "Starry Cove has seen a *significant* uptick in violent crime in the past few months. Coincidentally, there seems to be quite a lot of deaths when Poppy Lewis is nearby. Would you like to comment?"

I sank in my chair. She was doing it again. This reporter had pointed the finger at me last time and turned the town against me.

"No comment," said Deputy Todd.

"Here's a comment," Harper shouted, standing up. "Starry Cove is safer with Poppy in town. I speak from experience. And I *know* you know that this whole town knows what I'm talking about, *Miss Valentine*."

A burst of clapping and a few hoots flew up from the crowd. Veronica pursed her lips. Of course, she knew what Harper was talking about, since she'd once written an entire front-page article about how I had saved Harper's life—and caught a murderer in the process. The sound of the town's support gave me strength and reinforced my appreciation for my new home and its residents.

Deputy Todd shot her a smug grin. "Looks like your attempt to rile up the masses has failed, Miss Valentine. Better luck next time." He grabbed the notecard off the dais and left the stage, replaced by Mayor Jim.

"Settle down, thank you, everyone." Mayor Jim waved his hands in the air until everyone had settled in once again. "Now, let's get on to our next order of business—the upcoming election. As you all probably know, I am running unopposed once again, but that doesn't mean everyone shouldn't get into the spirit and tell your friends and families to come out and vote one week from today. I know I'll be there, and I hope to see all your wonderful faces too as we continue our unique Starry Cove tradition."

Harper leaned into Angie and me and whispered, "He acts like he's won already. Can you believe this guy?"

"He's unopposed," I reminded her. "You know what that means, right?"

"Yeah. It means after this, Dewey's going to hit the campaign trail."

"You cannot be serious," said Angie. "How can a cat even run for mayor?"

Harper glanced toward Dewey and our eyes followed. His lumpy orange shape had taken up a spot on the snack table nearest to the Town Hall office door. We watched as he smacked a cookie off the table with one paw, then dropped out of sight, presumably to kill, then devour it.

"Look at him. Little mayor-in-waiting is hanging out by his office already. He knows what's up." Harper turned back to me. "Poppy, are you in? Will you help me?"

I shrugged. "Sure, whatever you need."

"What about you Angie, little miss naysayer?"

"Fine. I'll help, but I don't know what you're planning on doing that could get a cat elected over the incumbent mayor."

"Watch and see." Harper hopped up and weaved in

and out of the chairs toward where Dewey had disappeared.

The town meeting had already ended, and Angie floated off to find Roy, leaving me alone in a row of empty seats. I spied Veronica headed my way, so I turned around and zig-zagged through the rows to the other side of the room. Glancing back, I saw that she was also dodging chairs and had closed the gap on me. Now I was trapped between the snack table and a thick crowd of people deep in conversation.

"Miss Lewis," Veronica called, panting as she reached me.

"What do you want?"

"I just want to ask you a few questions." She pulled out her recorder and shoved it a few inches from my face. "Now, what can you share with my readers about the day of Edgar Biggs's murder?"

"Nothing. I wasn't there, and I have no further comment."

She grabbed my arm as I tried to pass behind her. "But you found the body, didn't you? That must have been exciting."

I shook her hand off my arm and scowled. "Exciting?"

"I mean, it must have shaken you a little." She pushed the recorder even closer. "Or are you so used to dead bodies now that they don't faze you at all?" A glint twinkled in her eye.

Vile woman. "Whatever you're trying to trap me in, it won't work."

"Hey, reporter lady," came Harper's voice as she walked up to us with Dewey lazing like jelly in her arms.

"Leave Poppy alone. I've got a story for you right here."

Nine

I AWOKE THE next morning to repeated ringing of my doorbell. Wiping the sleep from my eyes, I shuffled from the air mattress to the front door and was surprised to find Harper, arms full of cardboard, butcher paper, and cans of paint. Dewey sat quietly on the rail post, watching with interest at Harper's flailing.

"Help me with all this," she said, shoving a bucket of paintbrushes into my arms. "I had to ring the doorbell with my nose."

"Who are you?" I scoffed. "You cannot be Harper since, according to my clock, it's barely seven in the morning."

"Your sarcasm can wait." Harper hurried into the house. "I've got some time before my rounds so I wanted to get started on Dewey's signs and campaign swag." She looked around for a place to set down the pile. "Where should I put all this?"

I quickly cleared the items off Dimitri's makeshift plywood and sawhorse table, and Harper dumped her armload in the middle, letting everything spill out at random. Dewey jumped onto the table and began sniffing at the paint cans.

"What did you have in mind?" I asked.

"First, I want to get some signs passed around town so people can put them up in their windows. I don't have the fancy waterproof material, so no lawn signs—wouldn't want Dewey's face to melt like Mayor Jim's did on his flyers."

"I'm going to need some coffee for this." I plodded toward the kitchen before remembering it was completely demolished and useless. Instead, I'd set up my coffee maker on a small table by the air mattress, easily accessible during the day and evening.

"Great idea—you make coffee and I'll get our painting stations set up."

Painting stations? Apparently, Harper was going to work me like an assembly line. Definitely going to need coffee for this. "Maybe I should call up my out-of-work reno crew and ask them to help."

I was half-joking, but Harper said, "Could you? Maybe Cho has time to help?"

"What is this about Cho?" I asked. "You seem very interested in what she's up to. Yesterday, at the bakery, you wanted to come with me and ask her questions, and you've been awfully defensive of her too."

Harper fiddled with the brushes. "What do you mean?"

"You know what I mean."

"All right, all right. Cho's just, you know, got an edge to her. She's a cool. Tattoos, that sort of thing."

My eyes narrowed. "You like her."

"So what if I do?" shot Harper.

"Nothing. Just that she may be a murderer."

"She's not a murderer. At least, I don't think so. I got a good vibe from her. We had... a moment—when you spilled your coffee the other morning like a clumsy ape. I got a vibe, okay?"

"Okay, but remember what's going on. Don't get all doe-eyed and forget what we're trying to accomplish."

"When have I ever been doe-eyed?" asked Harper, offended.

"Never mind." I filled a mug with fresh coffee and surveyed the table of supplies. "Tell me what I need to do here. What's the plan?"

"We need to make a few signs. One for the bakery, of course, and one for the diner too. I'll probably have to ask Ursula about the general store. Do you think the church is out of the question? Dewey's probably more devout than Jim, anyway."

"I'm not sure Pastor Basil would approve of political signs on church grounds."

"Hmm, probably right," Harper mused. "Anyway, I'm going to ask Shelby if I can throw a party at the diner tomorrow night to kick off Dewey's campaign. It should get the whole town excited. Everyone likes a party."

I picked up a brush and grabbed a piece of the cardboard. "What do you want on these?"

Harper stopped and turned, putting her hands up like a marquee. "I'm thinking of 'Do-we want Dewey? Yes!' in bold letters. What do you think?"

"Catchy. I'll start with that. What else?"

"I'm going to work on these buttons," said Harper. "I knew I'd find a use for this button maker one day."

We were hard at work on Dewey's campaign swag when the doorbell rang again followed by heavy knocking. Harper continued as I opened the front door. It was Mayor Jim, face hot as fire.

"I know she's here," he said.

"Who?"

"Don't play games. Harper Tillman."

Harper swaggered over to the door, paintbrush in hand. "Why, Mayor Jim, what a surprise," she said through a plastic smile. "How can I help you this morning?"

He held up a tightly rolled newspaper. "I know this is your doing."

"Is that my paper?" I asked.

"Yes, it is," he spat, slamming the newspaper into my hand.

I unrolled the paper and read the front-page headline: *Murder Strikes Starry Cove*. "You think Harper is a murderer?"

"Not that headline, the other one." He jabbed his finger toward the bottom of the page, annoyed.

I scanned the top page again, landing on another article closer to the bottom and I held it out so Harper and I could both read.

Valued Tomcat Vies for Votes

As time runs short in Starry Cove's mayoral race, a new challenger has entered the fray—ginger feline, Dewey. Fondly known as "Mayor Dewey" to the townsfolk, Dewey now hopes to make the title official. Local resident, Harper Tillman, shared the details with me in a *Vista View* exclusive interview.

Valentine: Miss Tillman, can you tell our readers why Dewey is running for office?

Tillman: Sure. Mayor Dewey's a Starry Cove treasure. He's trusted by the residents and likes to keep the town clear of vermin—he's just got one more rat to clear out. Vote for Dewey!

Valentine: Are you referring to the current mayor and until-recently unopposed incumbent, Mayor Jim Thornen?

Tillman: I sure am.

Valentine: And what are Dewey's policy platforms for this election?

Tillman: Naps for everyone and free fish on Fridays.

Valentine: I see. And does Dewey have anything to say about all this himself?

Tillman: He's napping right now, but when he wakes up, I'm sure he'll want to chat, as long as you pet him too.

"Awesome," said Harper. "I wasn't sure if she was going to publish it."

"So, you admit it!"

"Admit it? Sure I do. In fact, I've got to get going, these campaign signs won't put themselves up." Harper held up a freshly painted sign—Dew it for Dewey.

"That cat is a menace."

Harper's eyes narrowed. "Don't think I've forgotten the time you called animal control on him. He hasn't forgotten it either."

"You have turned this town into a mockery." He stamped his foot. "It will take us years to recover our reputation."

"Look Jim," said Harper, "I really appreciate your concern, but the only thing you need to worry yourself about now is finding a new job."

He gave Harper one final furious glare before turning tail and stomping down the stairs toward the street.

***

Harper eventually left for her rounds, taking most of the campaign items with her. I had the remainder of the morning to myself, but at midday set out to find Dimitri again. The guys at the bar said he frequented there around lunchtime, and by going at midday, I was hoping to catch him enjoying a beer and a sandwich.

As I drove up, it looked as vacant as it did during my previous visit, except now there was a truck out front with a logo on the doors that read "Dimitri's Drywall." Bingo.

I entered from the light into the darkness inside, quickly scanning the room for Dimitri. The guys at the bar must have recognized me since Gus shouted for me to join them.

"Hey there, Poppy," said Joe the bartender. "The Dodgers play at one. Did you come to root against them?"

I stepped up to the bar. "Not today, guys. Have you seen Dimitri? I'm still looking for him."

"Sure, he's in the back."

I turned to the back corner which was obstructed when I entered and saw Dimitri staring at me. He must have heard me say his name.

"Thanks guys." I headed to the table where Dimitri sat.

"What you want?" he asked in his heavy accent. He held his sandwich, half-eaten, in front of him. "I heard from these men that you come here looking for me. And now you are here again."

"I wanted to ask you about Edgar. I know it's probably not a good time—"

"Is not." He took a bite.

"—but I hoped you'd be able to help me. My renovation project has been shut down while the deputy sheriff investigates and, well, he isn't exactly the fastest or smartest on the force."

"I do not see how that my problem."

"Don't you want to get back to work?"

He took another bite of sandwich, chewing slowly before responding. "I have already talked to these sheriff people." He waved an arm dismissively. "Do not want to talk anymore."

Maybe I wouldn't get anything out of him. He didn't even sound like he wanted to come back to the project. I had to try another tactic.

"Someone mentioned that you and Edgar were friends."

"Not friends."

"Okay, but they said you came here—to this bar—together."

"We come to bar, we drink, we watch game. No

more."

"Did that stop when you found out Edgar was stealing from you?"

Dimitri took a long drink and clenched his jaw. "I not know what you think, lady, but I not kill Edgar."

"But it was your nail gun that killed him."

"Everyone use it. Everyone." Dimitri's Slavic accent thickened the more heated he got. "You not know what go on with that crew, okay?" He took another swig and set the glass next to three other empty pint glasses.

"Tell me then," I pleaded.

"Edgar was horrible person." His words slurred. "I see him take money out of my toolbox. I see this with my own eyes, okay?"

"Okay." My voice urged him to continue.

"He deny it completely. So now," Dimitri held up his hands, "he horrible person to me. That is story."

"If you didn't do it, like you say, then who do you think did?"

"I not know. I just feel sorry for his kids, okay? Kids love him very much. And he love them. Good kids."

"You can't think of anyone who would want to hurt Edgar?" I asked.

"Everyone want to hurt Edgar, okay? That is problem."

"And you must have wondered about your nail gun."

"I tell you, everyone use nail gun, especially Blister and twins. Even Edgar use it. He not shoot himself, did he?"

I hadn't considered that possibility before. Had Edgar shot himself in the head with the nail gun? But that wouldn't explain what he was doing in my closet. I shook off the thought. "No, I suppose not."

"You want to know who to talk to? You talk to Blister, okay? Blister think Edgar want to steal his business. They fight about it—I hear them. I hear Blister say he going to kill Edgar."

"Kill him?" I repeated, shocked.

"Yes," he said, taking another drink. "Kill him."

"And you told the sheriff this too?"

"Yes. I tell you I already talk to them, okay?"

Things were not looking good for Blister. As much as I wanted to believe it, and as much as I wanted to support Angie, Blister was looking more and more like the prime suspect. And it grated on me that Deputy Todd might actually be right. But I had one last question in me for Dimitri—one last question to rule him out completely.

"Where were you at the end of that workday when Blister sent everyone home? Someone said they couldn't find you."

"You tell me who say this," he demanded, slamming his glass down on the table. "You say 'someone,' now you tell me who."

"What's going on over there?" Joe peered over while wiping a plate dry with a dirty rag. "You two all right?"

Dimitri stood up from the table, "Yes," he spat. "We all right." He gathered his pack from the side chair and stormed out of the bar. The harsh daylight streaming in as he opened the bar door caused me to wince and look away.

Interesting, I thought. *Very interesting.*

Ten

ANGIE AND I had promised Harper we'd meet at my house that night to work on Dewey's campaign party decorations. I made a fresh pot of coffee and laid out some store-bought cheese and crackers on my crate-table for a snack.

"Oh good," said Angie. "I'm glad you got something other than baked goods. I'm starting to build an aversion."

"I thought you were going to hire some help at the bakery?"

"I am, I just haven't gotten to it yet—it's been too crazy to get any help to help with the craziness."

"Why doesn't Roy do it? What does he do, anyway?"

"I know you don't see it—"

A knock sounded at the door. "That must be Harper." I opened the door and Harper walked in with Dewey cradled in her arms. He wore a little party hat with an elastic chin cord. Harper had painted a big 'MD' on the front in bright blue letters.

"Run along, little guy," she said, setting him down.

She grabbed the hat off him just as he skittered off somewhere deep in the house. Harper turned to Angie and me, standing by the worktable. "We've been canvassing the town. Numbers look good."

"What numbers?" Angie scoffed.

"The polling numbers, Angie. Dewey's coming out of the gate strong."

"I put up a sign in my window, but I don't know what else you want me to do."

"Thanks, that's all we need—your unwavering support."

Angie rolled her eyes. "What are we doing tonight, anyway? I have an early bedtime, remember?"

Harper pulled out a stack of postcards from her bag. "We're going to be addressing and stamping these. I had a few made in Vista today."

"A few?" Angie gaped at the stack.

"That's right, one for every voter in Starry Cove. Look," she said, holding out a small stamper. "I had these made so we can give the postcards a polished look. It's got Dewey's face on it."

"How much money have you spent on this campaign?" I asked.

"Don't worry about it. It's all for a good cause. Anyway, while we're doing these, you can tell us what you found out today. You mentioned you were headed back to the Vista Tavern."

"I found Dimitri."

"You did?" asked Angie. "What happened?"

"He was pretty shifty, and he'd been drinking a lot."

"Drowning his guilt?" Harper wondered.

"I'm not sure. He confirmed that everyone used his

tools, so I don't think the fact that it was his nail gun that killed Edgar is any type of sticking point anymore—everyone used it."

"Not Blister, though," said Angie, nibbling a cracker.

"Well, Dimitri did say that Blister used the nail gun too." I braced myself for the next revelation. "And he said that Blister and Edgar had been fighting."

Angie looked shocked. "I don't believe it."

"And he said Blister threatened to kill Edgar."

"That's impossible." Angie shook her head. "He's lying to cover up his own guilt." She exchanged looks with Harper, then me. "Right?"

"It's not looking good, Angie." She began to interrupt me, but I held up a hand. "I don't believe Blister is guilty, but I'm also finding it hard to defend him when there are so many accusations thrown his way."

"Don't worry, Angie," said Harper, giving her a squeeze. "We'll figure it out. Until then, let's get started on these postcards."

After stamping and personalizing what seemed like a thousand sheets of cardstock, the three of us finally slumped on the old sofa. We sat in silence admiring the stack of cards, ready to be distributed the next day to each resident of Starry Cove. My eyes drifted to the chaos surrounding us—the half-finished walls, the plastic sheeting, piles of rubbish in every corner. "What do you two think Arthur would make of all this, if he could see us now?"

"He'd love it," said Angie. "He knew you'd do right by the place."

"Yeah. Arthur loved this old house, and now you do too. You're just showing it some extra love right now. Do you think Arthur would have voted for Dewey?"

Angie smiled. "In a heartbeat. You know he would."

This made me smile. My two friends knew Arthur much better than I ever had. I'd barely known it him at all. I tapped my chin. "What about what Greta said? I'm still wondering what she and Arthur were working on together."

"You said you took pictures of the notebook with your phone," said Harper. "Let's see them."

I pulled my phone out of my back pocket and started flipping through the pictures. Harper leaned in on one side and Angie leaned in on the other as we perused each page together.

"This might be where you remember seeing the symbol, Harper." I showed her the last page of the notebook, with the symbol highlighted starkly in the center of the page.

"Maybe. I feel like there were more things around it, more embellishment or shading or something."

"Here's the map again." I flipped the phone pictures back to the page we'd discovered when we first pulled the book out of Arthur's secret hiding place.

Angie squinted. "It's so hard to read. Can you zoom in?"

"It still looks like a treasure map to me," said Harper. "And there's that notation we saw when we first found the book 'find P byway the line'—whatever that means."

"Remember what Greta said? She said they were working on a project about the surrounding area, so maybe this is a map of something nearby."

"I have no idea what it might be a map of." Angie slumped back into the sofa. "None of this makes any sense to me."

"It says we're supposed to find P, obviously," said Harper, shrugging. "But I'm as lost as you two."

Angie was right, the entire notebook was a jumble of seemingly random scribbles and jottings, few of which made any sense to the casual reader.

I dropped the phone to my lap, defeated. "It's as if they wrote the entire thing in code or shorthand, not meant to be deciphered by anyone other than the author."

"That means Greta's the only one who knows what any of this means," said Harper. "I wish we knew what Arthur knew."

I sat upright. "Maybe we can."

"What do you mean?"

"Well, Greta said she and Arthur were researching this topic, whatever it was. Maybe Arthur had some other related books. You know, reference material."

"Where are Arthur's books now? You've had the whole house packed away."

"His books are in the basement. I moved the smaller items down there—only the big furniture is in storage."

"The basement..." said Angie, wringing her hands. "I don't like it down there."

"Me neither," I said. "It still gives me chills, but

unless we want to haul all the boxes of books up the stairs to go through them, we've got to spend some time down there."

Harper groaned.

"Don't you want to find out what this notebook is about?"

"Yes, but I also don't want to go down to your creepy basement."

"Don't be such a pansy. You either, Angie. This could be our best opportunity to figure it out."

I stood up from the couch and headed into my demolished kitchen. Harper and Angie followed close behind. The door to the basement was in the far corner and the rickety steps traveled down, underneath the bigger stairwell that led to the second floor above.

Harper held out a hand to stop me. "Hold on. I'm not going down there with your pathetic flashlights." She grabbed one of the large spotlights left by the construction crew, along with a long extension cord. "This should be enough light. Angie, plug that in, would you?"

Angie plugged the extension cord into the wall socket closest to the basement door. The spotlight blinded us as it flashed on.

"Yeah," I said, blinking. "That should work. Be careful on these stairs now that none of us can see anything but spots."

I'd placed all the boxes of books against the nearest wall, not too far into the basement. Avoiding the depths of the basement had become second nature by now, ever since the three of us had discovered Arthur's secret hiding spot. A bookcase now covered the hole in the wall so as not to arouse any more suspicion while the renovation crew was on site.

"Here," I said at the foot of the stairs. "These big boxes are all of Arthur's books. Just browse the spines and see if anything jumps out at you. Anything that might have to do with the area around Starry Cove."

"There must be a thousand books here," Harper wailed. She set down the spotlight and faced it toward the ceiling, filling the entire space with plenty of light for the job ahead.

"Pipe down. Angie and I just stamped a thousand and one postcards, so you can find the energy to rifle through some books."

Angie sat on the bottom step of the stairwell and Harper and I sat cross-legged on the dusty floor. We each grabbed a box and began shoveling through, looking for anything of interest. Arthur's taste was eclectic, he had books on psychology, butterflies, Zoroastrianism—even a comic book from the 1960s.

"I'm not having any luck. Are you guys?"

Angie shook her head and blew the dust off the spine of an old dictionary. "Nothing so far."

"Wait," said Harper. "I think I found something." She held up the book which looked about as uninteresting as a book could be—brown linen cover, brown lettering on the spine. The book could easily get lost or overlooked on anyone's shelf, eyes simply glancing over it as though it didn't exist at all.

"Doesn't look like much," said Angie.

Harper opened to the title page. "*History of Starry Cove 1800-1900* by Professor Emeril Slatherby." She flipped to the table of contents and perused the options as Angie and I returned to our own searches.

"Ah-ha!" Harper jabbed a thin finger to a spot on the opened page. "There's a bit about your house in here, Poppy."

"Really?" I scooted over to peer inside the book.

"Yeah, it says the house was built in 1881 by Claude Goodwin and was one of the first Queen Anne style Victorians built on the west coast."

"That's pretty cool," said Angie. "It should be on the list of historic places, shouldn't it?"

"But it's not," I said. "Otherwise, I would have received a lot more pushback on the renovation plans."

"That's strange. I wonder why?"

I took the book from Harper and read further along. "It also says here that the house was known as Pearl-by-the-Sea because it was so magnificent in its day."

"Still is," said Angie.

"There's more," I said excitedly. "Claude Goodwin was the great-grandson of suspected pirate Atticus Goodwin."

Harper's eyes bugged out. "Whoa, that is something."

I continued reading from the book.

> Starry Cove's history as a pirate shelter in the early nineteenth century has been well documented. Pirates navigated into the cove by starlight, steered by their comrades on the shore who waved torches to guide them into the shelter of the harbor and avoid the dangerous rocks nearby. The seclusion of the cove

made it a favorite of the smaller pirate vessels that operated during the heyday of Pacific coast piracy, which spanned 1750-1800.

Atticus Goodwin, more commonly known as Gold Tooth Goodwin, frequented the cove during the years 1785 to October 1790, when reports indicate his ship, the Jolly Jenny, was scuttled in an early season storm. All hands were lost, but rumors swirled that Atticus Goodwin—now aged over fifty—had survived, and intentionally dashed his ship on the rocks in an attempt to disappear with a recently cached haul of Mexican gold pilfered from Spanish settlements lining the coast.

"Gold doubloons," shouted Harper. "I knew we'd finally find something good. This must be what Arthur and Greta were after? The pages in that notebook look like a treasure map, right? And here's our treasure, right here in this book."

"But this was over *two hundred* years ago," said Angie. "That Atticus fellow sounds like bad news, but what about Claude Goodwin? He built this lovely mansion."

"With hot Mexican gold, no doubt." Harper clapped her dusty hands and let out a holler. "What do we do with this info?"

"Well, we need to do something. Greta said people

would be after the notebook—and now we know what *might* be in it." I gave Harper a stern look. It would do no good to get excited over a mere possibility. We had to keep our wits about us.

"What if Greta is the one after it? She already tried to take the notebook from you."

"And what if she was telling the truth?" I asked. "We need to watch our steps from now on. The notebook might be safely locked up in Vista, but someone could be watching us. We can't just prance around talking about pirates and treasure."

Harper huffed. "I wasn't going to prance around."

"It's been a long time since I've pranced," said Angie. "I don't know if I'm even capable anymore."

"I'm going to lock this book in Vista too—it seems important. But I want to read the whole thing first. There could be more clues."

"Does that mean we can leave the basement?" asked Angie. "Are we done here?"

"Yeah, let's go," Harper picked up the work lamp. "Isn't it past your bedtime, Angie?"

"Very funny," Angie said, yawning. "I guess I am pretty tired."

"C'mon." I led us up the stairs. "I've got some reading to do."

Eleven

I FELL ASLEEP before finishing the book that night, so when I woke up on the air mattress, I slid off and made myself a pot of coffee right away. It was a beautiful morning, and the fog burnt off early, leaving the sun shining as I enjoyed the coffee on the porch with Mayor Dewey.

"Do you even want to be mayor?" I asked him.

Dewey blinked up at me before flopping on my slippered foot, using it to scratch his back.

I heard Deputy Todd's boots before I saw him. I thought about slipping quickly and quietly into the house, but his eyes homed in on me as soon as he came onto the roundabout.

"How's the investigation going?" I called to him as he approached the porch. "I'd like to continue the work on my house at some point."

"I understand, Miss Lewis," he said in his twangy drawl. "Now, you wouldn't have happened to have been snooping around Vista at say, the Vista Tavern, now would you? After I explicitly told you to stay out of this investigation."

I took a long sip of coffee. "It's not illegal to go to a bar, is it, Deputy?"

"Well, no." He leaned back on his heels a bit. "Just seems like an odd place for you to go. Rough place."

"They have great sandwiches."

Deputy Todd stared me down, but I didn't flinch, then he grumbled something under his breath.

"Do you have anything else to share? Am I free to continue renovating the house yet?"

"Unfortunately, I have an update on that."

"What do you mean by 'unfortunately'?"

"Well, we found everyone's prints on the murder weapon—including Edgar's—so that was a dead end. Pardon the pun." He took another moment before continuing, "It looks like you'll have to find a new general contractor."

"Why's that?" I sat up, concerned.

"Because as of seven o'clock this morning, I've arrested Blister Hauser on suspicion of murder."

"That's ridiculous." Dewey meowed in annoyance as I stood up and he scampered off into the bushes. "Blister couldn't have done it. *Wouldn't* have done it."

"It may be news to you, but it appears Edgar was planning to start a competing business. Seems Blister wasn't too happy with that. There's your motive, bright as the midday sun."

"It's not possible—he has an alibi. He was at the hardware store, remember? Trevor French would have seen him."

"Yes, I remember. Except, when I tried to talk to

Trevor, turns out he'd left the very night of the murder for a two-week sight-seeing trip to the Costa Rican jungle, so he's conveniently unavailable for questioning—or to confirm Mr. Hauser's alibi. Now, I ask you, what kind of businessman doesn't get receipts? Blister's got no alibi to speak of."

"There's got to be something else," I pleaded. "What about surveillance video?"

"Surveillance video?" He stared at me as though I'd sprouted a second head. "This is Starry Cove—nobody's got surveillance video."

"But Angie will be devastated."

"Sorry, Miss Lewis. Looks like your general contractor will be behind bars for a while, and the only other one I can think of is dead with a nail gun in his forehead."

***

Stepping into the bakery was hard enough, just knowing I'd have to tell Angie about Blister. It was even harder once I saw the exuberance on her face.

"Good morning, Poppy," she chirped, bustling around behind the bakery counter.

"Uh, hi Angie."

"Cinnamon roll?" She held up a plate, steam escaping from the hot treat she'd already prepared for me. "Coffee?"

"Yes, please," I said, taking the plate. "What's going on? You're awfully cheerful this morning."

"Roy and I have a few people coming in today for interviews. It will be so nice to get some more help around here."

The sound of faint rock music and clanging trays wafted from the back kitchen. Roy must be hard at work backstage.

"Look, Angie. I've got—"

"And one of them has bakery experience already. Can you believe it? I guess a little shop in Vista closed down and my job opening came at the right time."

"That's great."

"Once I get more help in here, I can help you with investigating Edgar's murder—and help Blister."

"Right, about Blister—"

"Oh, I forgot to tell you!" Angie clapped her pudgy hands together. "There's a magazine—well, a trade magazine—that wants to do an article about small town bakeries, and they've asked me to be in it. I'm so excited—this could really put our bakery on the map." She did a twirl and stamped her feet.

"Wow, this is all great news." I was now even more reluctant to tell Angie about Blister. But the band-aid had to come off. "Angie, I just got through talking with Deputy Todd."

"Oh?" She continued to hum and bustle around the bakery.

I steeled myself. "He said that Blister was arrested this morning for Edgar's murder."

Her round face popped up from the pastry case she'd been cleaning, her smile turned to a frown. "He what? No." She shook her head. "No. Blister is innocent."

"I know Angie, but—"

She wailed, eyes watering. "What are we going to do? We've got to clear his name. I know he couldn't have done this." Angie had now broken down into fits of tears.

I ran over and wrapped her in a hug, trying my best to comfort someone who's always comforting others.

"I'm going to figure it out, Angie. I promise."

"Oh Poppy." She wept into my shoulder.

"I have a few ideas. I still haven't been able to talk to Dustin and Justin. No one seems to know where they are. But they owe loads of people money, and that sounds like a motive to me."

"It wasn't Blister—can't they see that?" Tears dribbled down her cheeks. "It had to be one of the others."

The door to the bakery swung open and Harper appeared in dark sunglasses, her arms and hands loaded with Dewey campaign swag, signs, and flyers. A trail of ribbon floated behind her and got stuck in the door.

"I already talked to Shelby. She's agreed to host the kickoff party tonight." Harper set a pile of flyers on the small table just inside the bakery. "Phew. Why the long faces?"

"They've arrested Blister," I said.

"What?" Harper gaped, dropping the rest of the items onto the chair, some falling to the floor. She rushed over to Angie and gave her a bear hug. Harper was so much taller than Angie she leaned over into the hug, completely enveloping Angie in her long spindly arms. "Angie, I'm so sorry."

"Thanks Harper. I've had a big cry and I don't want to be a baby, but we know Blister is innocent—we just need to prove it."

I patted Angie on the arm. "We will. Don't worry about it—focus on your interviews today."

"Oh right, you've got interviews. I won't crowd the bakery with Dewey's stuff then. Poppy, can I keep it at your place? It's still closer to the diner than mine."

"Sure."

"And would you mind taking a few of these flyers with you today? I assume you'll be snooping around some more. It's against Post Office rules for me to campaign on my rounds, otherwise I'd carry a bunch too. Here," she said, handing me a stack, "you take these."

Dewey's furry ginger face took up almost the entire flyer. The words "Dew your Duty, Vote for Dewey" read boldly along the bottom.

"Can I leave some here, Angie?"

"Okay, but leave them on the table."

"And will you put up another campaign sign?" Harper held up one sign we'd painted previously—Vote Fur Dewey.

Angie sighed. "Fine, put it in the window, but don't obstruct any of my pastries."

We broke soon after to head off on our separate tasks for the day. My focus would be on acquitting Blister. The memory of Deputy Todd's smug face and Angie's tears spurred me on.

***

The town church was a quick walk down Main Street from the bakery. Along the way I spotted Lovie headed in the same direction. I rushed to catch up with her, slowing down only as I reached her side.

"Good morning, Poppy," she said, now slowing her stride.

"Off to the church this morning?"

"Yes. As you know, I spend a lot of time volunteering. Today is no different."

"And I'm sure Pastor Basil appreciates all the time and effort you put in."

Lovie stopped abruptly, forcing me to halt as well. "You want something from me, don't you?"

I cut the niceties. "I do want something. I'm looking for information."

"Go on." She eyed me sideways.

"I was hoping you may have seen something the other day—the morning Edgar Biggs was murdered. Maybe you remember if anyone went into the hardware store?"

"Why would I know if anyone went to the hardware store?"

"Well, you see everything around town…"

Lovie put both hands on her hips. "I most certainly do not see everything around town."

"So, you didn't see anyone?"

Her lips twitched. "I may have seen someone go in, but I couldn't say who it was since I was watching from the window in the diner."

"But you saw *someone*?"

"Yes, I just said I did."

I clapped my hands together. "Lovie, that's great news."

"I'm glad you're happy," she replied, continuing down the sidewalk, "but I need to get to church."

"I'll walk with you—I'm headed there too."

The steeple was always the first thing to come into view, then the small stone non-denominational Fellowship of Faith church with its luscious and well-tended garden. If I knew anything, it was that we would probably find Pastor Basil Meyers somewhere in that garden. Sure enough, as Lovie and I approached, we spotted him on one of the stone benches that dotted the garden surrounding the church. His eyes were closed, his face turned toward the sun. He sat cross-legged on the bench and his sandals sat neatly on the ground in front of him. Un-rimmed glasses perched on the end of his long nose and a tie-dyed shirt peek through from under his wool sweater.

"Good morning," I said, coming up the walkway from the road.

"Good morning, Pastor," said Lovie in passing as she continued toward the church door. "I'm going straight inside."

"Good morning to you both." His eyes remained closed. "Morning's light brings purpose bright."

"Sorry?"

"It means, the morning illuminates our purpose for the day."

"Does it?" I was still confused.

He smiled and nodded his head. "What can I do for you, Poppy?"

"I assume you heard about the death of Edgar Biggs?"

He nodded, eyes still closed. "It's a real bummer. Always sad to lose one of God's creatures. I understand he had young children."

"Yes, two. Anyway, I'm trying to help a friend who's in trouble and I was hoping you might be able to assist me."

He finally broke from his meditation and looked at me. "How so?"

"I've been tracking down what happened to my

renovation crew that day, and I thought you may have seen Blister—I mean, Bill—Hauser."

Pastor Basil stared at me for a moment, thinking. "I can't say I remember seeing Blister at all for the past few days, but I did see someone who I thought was working on your house."

"You did?"

"Yeah, I think her name was Cho. I saw her at the diner the other day."

"But you didn't see Blister at all?"

He spread out his hands as if to say sorry.

"Is Bea inside?"

"Sure is. Every day, like clockwork."

"Thanks." I pulled out one of the flyers. "Here's a flyer for tonight's campaign kick-off party for Dewey." Mayor Dewey was a frequent visitor to the church garden and was often found rolling around in the dirt and chasing butterflies. I thought the pastor might be a good ally.

"Little rascal," Pastor Basil said, shaking his head in amusement. "Who knew he had it in him?"

"Apparently Harper did," I said and headed into the church to find Bea.

Just through the doors the sound of the bells rang beautifully in my ears. Bea stood at the front of the church by a small table with each of the various bells lined up neatly in a row. Beatrice Trotter, a meek, middle-aged shell of a woman, was a member of the church's bell choir, and a devoted member of the Fellowship of Faith. She was also married to one of the worst men in town—Kenny Trotter. In fact, I believed she spent so much time at church so she could be away from Kenny as much as possible.

I waited for her practice to end, then called out to her. She smiled and joined me at a pew in the front.

"Hi Poppy," she said, sitting down.

"How are you doing, Bea? I hope I'm not disturbing you."

"Oh no." She waved a hand. "I'm always practicing. And Pastor Basil says the bells help him when he's writing his sermons."

"They sound lovely. Truly inspiring, I'm sure."

"Anyway, I'm here all day, mostly. Kenny drops me off and I get a ride back with Georgia in the evenings. Kenny doesn't like to stay in town much, ever since, you know…"

I nodded. Kenny was on my naughty list from a few months ago, and I wouldn't show my face in Starry Cove if I were him, either. "I was hoping you might be able to help me."

"However I can. I feel so bad about what happened, you know, before…"

I nodded again. "I don't suppose you were anywhere near the hardware store last Tuesday, when that man, Edgar, died at my house."

"Oh," she said, pained. "That was so sad. I wish I could help you, but I didn't go to the hardware store. I was here at church most of the day."

I knew it was a long shot, but I was still disappointed. I was ready to thank her and move on, but she continued after a moment. "Now that I think of it, I did stop at the pharmacy next door to the hardware store for my prescription—I do like that new pharmacist." She smiled, and quickly added, "Although Arthur was wonderful." She patted my arm, knowing Arthur had been my uncle.

"You may want to talk to Ursula. When I got there, the general store was closed for lunch. I waited for Ursula to come back since she's in the bell choir and I wanted to speak with her about tomorrow's service. When she arrived, I think she mentioned that she'd come from the hardware store."

This got my attention and I perked up. "She did?" I wondered if this was who Lovie had seen.

"Yes, now that I recall, she mentioned she'd been at the housewares store during that lunch break."

"That's fantastic—thank you, Bea." I gave her a hug which surprised her. She must have thought I was crazy getting so excited over Ursula's trip to the housewares store. I stood up, ready to rush to the general store, but stopped myself.

"Here." I handed her a flyer. "We're having a party at the diner tonight. Everyone is welcome."

"Thank you," she said, staring at the flyer in confusion as I rushed out of the church.

***

I burst into the general store, jangling the bells that announced customers arriving and leaving. I spotted Ursula stacking boxed merchandise along a wall shelf behind the counter.

"Ursula," I shouted, startling her.

She gasped and spun around. "You scared me to death, Poppy. I thought I was being robbed." She wiped a strand of brown hair out of her eyes and pinched it back into her ponytail, securing it away from her face.

"Sorry. I need to know if you saw Blister at the hardware store during lunch on Tuesday."

Ursula, still recovering from her near-heart attack, took a moment to process my words. "The hardware store…"

"Yes, Trevor's hardware store." I leaned over the counter at her. "Bea told me that you were there picking something up during the lunch hour on Tuesday. It's very important that you remember."

"Okay… I guess I was there."

"Do you know who Blister Hauser is?"

"Oh sure, I know Blister."

"Did you see him there?" I demanded.

Ursula took one step back from the counter, farther away from me.

"Sorry, Ursula." I took a deep breath to calm myself down. "It's just really urgent that you remember if you saw him or not."

"Well, now, let's see." She stared off into the distance, walking the events through her mind. "I went over to the hardware store to pick up some gardening gloves. I walked in and went straight to that little lazy Susan near the front—the one with all the gardening tools with floral handles—but I don't remember seeing anyone and I was only there for a few minutes."

I let out a sigh. Not the words I wanted to hear.

"But I think I may have *heard* someone in the very back row. I don't remember seeing who it was though. After that, I went up to Trevor and checked out."

"You heard someone though? That's great."

"It is? But I don't know who."

"At least someone was there."

Ursula shrugged.

"Hello ladies," Ryan said, walking up to us. "Are you

all right, Poppy?" He looked closer at my face. I must have been all red from the effort and excitement.

"Yes, I'm fine."

"Good. I'm glad you stopped in. A strange little old woman came by yesterday asking about Arthur. I thought you'd want to know."

My eyes narrowed. "Was she scraggly looking? Like a hag?"

"Aye. Although I wouldn't go as far as to call her a hag. That's a bit much, isn't it?"

"Maybe," I said dryly. "Did she ask about anything else?"

"As a matter of fact, she did. She wanted to know if Arthur left any personal notes or documents here at the pharmacy."

"And what did you tell her?"

"I told her no—there was nothing here when I arrived except patient records and the inventory."

"Good."

"Do you know who she was? It sounds like you aren't too pleased with her coming around."

I pulled Ryan aside, out of earshot of Ursula, who'd returned to packing the shelves.

"She came by the house the other day after you left. Claimed to be a friend of Arthur's, but I'm not so sure. Now she's poking around here asking about his personal items. I don't like it."

"I see. I'll keep an eye out then."

"Thanks. How's the gazebo going? It should be done by now, right?"

"It took Quentin an extra half day, but it's finished, and it looks great. You should come over and see it. In fact, come over and we can have dinner tonight. A sort of ribbon-cutting, if you will."

I was about to say yes, but then I remembered Mayor Dewey's party. "I'd love to, Ryan, but we're having a party tonight for Dewey's campaign." I handed him a flyer.

"Aye. I saw the article yesterday. I'll see you there tonight, then. How about Sunday for dinner?"

I frowned. "Sunday is girls' night with Harper and Angie."

"Monday?" he asked, losing hope.

Finally, I could smile. "Yes, Monday sounds great."

"Excellent. Why don't you come over around seven and I'll have dinner ready?"

"Sounds great—"

Harper barreled through the door carrying a Dewey sign, nearly crashing into me and Ryan. "Oh good, you're here. Have you told these two about the party?"

"Just Ryan so far."

"I will be there with bells on," he said.

"Great, Mayor Dewey really likes bells. I'm officially on break, so I brought over a sign for the window." Harper held it up proudly—Dewey Want Change?—before striding up to Ursula at the counter.

I turned to Ryan. "I'll see you tonight at the party. With Harper in charge, it's sure to be a good one."

Twelve

HARPER CAME BY the house after her shift and we hauled all the material over to the diner to prepare for the party. We must have been a sight—two women burdened with streamers and balloons and signs and all sorts of colorful decorations.

"Good heavens, dearies," said Shelby as we tried to fit in the door of the diner. "Mason," she hollered at the squeaky red-headed teenager. "Go help them."

Mason shuffled over and took a few of the items out of our hands. Once in the safety of the diner, we let the balloons go, and they floated up to the ceiling, their ribbon tails dangling within arm's reach.

"Good," said Harper. "At least those will be out of our way for a while. Shelby, where can we put the rest of this down?"

"Oh, just set it on the counter. But get it up quick, I don't want to lose any customers."

Angie clamored in a few minutes later. "I saw you guys go by, but Roy and I were on our last interview of the day."

"How'd they go," I asked.

"Good, I think we'll bring on at least one of them—that one from Vista."

"That's great. Now you'll have more time to help with Dewey's campaign."

"He's not starting that soon, Harper. We still need to work out the laws and things."

"I can help you there, dearie," said Shelby. "You should talk to my lawyer—she's great."

"That'd be fantastic—thanks Shelby."

"What do you guys think?" Harper held up a sign over the counter. "Higher?"

That was just the beginning of our hour-long decorating chore. I was exhausted by the end of it, and the party had not even started. We guzzled three runs of the coffee maker to keep us going.

Lovie was the first to arrive and huddled with Shelby in the corner, watching us finish setting up. The rest of the town slowly trickled in and mingled at the snack table Shelby had set up near the entrance.

I leaned in close to Harper as we strung streamers in the far corner. "Word-of-mouth must have spread the news of the party quickly."

"I just had to tell Lovie. I knew she'd do the work for me after that."

"Work smarter, not harder," said Angie, and we all chuckled.

I looked around to make sure we were alone. "Now that I have you two away from the others, I want to update you on what I found out today."

"Please tell me you found out something good," said

Angie.

"Sort of. Turns out Ursula was at the hardware store about the same time as Blister."

Angie gasped. "Did she see him?"

"Well, no. All she said was she heard someone in the back aisle. But that's something at least."

"Okay, enough decorations." Harper stepped off the ladder. "Let's schmooze."

"Where's Mayor Dewey?"

"Oh no," said Harper. "I left him napping on your porch. I'll be right back." Harper dipped out of the diner and sprinted down the street. A larger crowd had arrived by the time she returned a few minutes later, the man—or cat—of the hour in her arms.

A raucous cheer arose as Dewey entered the room, and he blinked a few times, but otherwise didn't seem too affected by the noise and crowd. Harper set him down on the snack table and he promptly started playing with a ribbon dangling from a balloon overhead.

"What a great turnout," I said to Harper as she walked over to Angie and me.

"Great turnout. Better than I'd hoped for. There are some notable absences, mainly Mayor Jim, but no surprise there."

"There're a few others missing," said Angie. "But I guess we couldn't expect everyone to make it."

As we were talking, I saw a tiny figure enter the diner. Her blonde bob cut like a knife and her red-rimmed glasses gave her away at a hundred paces—Veronica Valentine.

"Look, that reporter's here. Did you contact her, Harper?"

"I did, but I only left a message. I didn't think she'd actually show up."

"She's headed this way. I don't like that lady." Angie huddled behind us, pretending to fix a streamer that had come loose.

"Hello ladies," Veronica said, recorder in hand. "Fine party you have going here."

Harper beamed. "Thank you. I wasn't sure you'd be able to make it."

"I got your message, then I received another call from Lovie Newman. I figured if she knew about it, everyone else would and, well, here we are."

"Dewey's at the snack table if you'd like to take a walk?" Harper led Veronica away, leaving Angie and I to breathe a sigh of relief.

"Didn't sound like she was here to ruin the party," said Angie. "I can never tell."

We let Harper take the lead—we were just there for moral support and ended up chatting to residents who sounded supportive of Dewey's campaign. Mayor Jim, it appeared, was less popular than I'd guessed. Most wore Mayor Dewey pins or ribbons and nibbled on cookies shaped like cats.

Angie elbowed me. "There's Ryan. How are things going with him?"

"We're having dinner on Monday. At his place." I winked and Angie giggled and clapped her hands.

"He's coming over."

"I had no idea Dewey was so popular," he said after wading through the crowd and reaching us in the back.

"Oh yeah," said Angie. "Everyone loves him. Except Jim, I think."

"I'm going to check out the refreshments. I'll see you on Monday, Poppy."

"See you then. Thanks for coming by," I said, smiling as he walked away.

"My, my." Angie looked up at me and batted her eyelashes dramatically. "You two are so cute together. Dinner should be interesting. Just the two of you, you said?"

"Hush." I tried to brush it off, but found it difficult to hold back my smile.

About an hour into the party, it surprised me to see Cho walk through the diner door. Harper spotted her immediately and gave her a wave. Cho smiled back warmly and headed straight to the refreshments table.

Deputy Todd, too, eventually showed up, but when I approached him, he said, "I'm only here to support Lovie. As a public figure it would be inappropriate for me to endorse one candidate over another."

"That's all well and good, but do you have any more news about the investigation?"

"Well, Blister maintains his innocence."

"Of course he does," Angie said storming up, a crumbled cookie in her hand. "Because he *is* innocent."

"Now, Mrs. Owens, settle down."

I chimed in with the only useful fact I knew at this point. "Ursula said she was at the hardware store at lunchtime and she heard someone else there."

Deputy Todd's eyebrows rose. "Oh yeah, who?"

Confound this man, why couldn't he just run with it. "Somebody—she's not sure who—just that there was someone else there besides her and Trevor."

"Thank you for that insightful tip, Miss Lewis.

Unfortunately, 'somebody, not sure who' isn't going to clear Blister Hauser."

"Could we come and talk to him? Maybe tomorrow? If he saw Ursula, wouldn't that put two and two together?"

Deputy Todd pursed his lips. "There's visiting hours in the morning, if you want to."

"We want to," Angie said quickly.

"All right, do whatever you want, but don't put ideas in his head." He stepped away from us. "I'm going to get a cookie."

I gnashed my teeth. It's as though he'd already tried Blister and discarded any chance of innocence. "That man will accept nothing less than an eyewitness."

Angie stared up at me, her eyes watering. "But how do we find out who was inside the hardware store?"

I struggled to answer her, but then it hit me—I had most of the town at my disposal right here. "We ask the masses, Angie." I stepped up onto one of the booth benches.

"Hand me that balloon and a fork," I said to her. I waited for a lull in the crowd noise then punctured the balloon. The pop was enough to startle the crowd and their faces turned our way in the corner.

"Everyone, can I have your attention," I shouted. Harper had eased her way through the crowd and started eyeing me, unsure of what I was doing since I hadn't planned to speak at Dewey's campaign party. "I want to ask if anyone remembers being at the hardware store on Tuesday? Does anyone remember seeing Blister Hauser at the hardware store?"

Faces turned to one another and there was a

collective mumbling, but no voices rang out. No one there had seen Blister.

Dejected, I stepped off the bench. "Sorry Angie."

We carried on with the party. Angie and I discussed visiting Blister tomorrow, and Harper continued to canvass the diner, urging anyone and everyone to vote for Dewey for mayor. No one gave any notice to the bell ringing above the door until a voice boomed through the room.

"This is a complete and utter farce!" yelled Mayor Jim.

"What are you doing here?" Harper shot back. "This party is for Mayor Dewey."

"*Mayor* Dewey? This is ridiculous. Look at yourselves, people—you're voting for a cat." His eyes scanned the room, then he pointed as he finally spotted Dewey. "There, him." Dewey blinked. "That's who you want as your mayor? A mangy, flea-bitten scamp?"

"Of course we don't," shouted Harper. "We already have one of those." A roar sprang from the crowd, hoots and hollers of laughter.

Mayor Jim fumed. "I won't let you turn this town into a laughingstock." He stomped to the nearest Dewey poster that we'd taped to a window and ripped it down, tossing it to the floor.

"Hey! You can't do that."

"Jim," Deputy Todd snarled, striding over to him. He grabbed Mayor Jim by the arm to stop him from ripping down another poster. "Time to leave, now. Before you cause more damage to Miss Shelby's diner."

"You'll all regret this," he shouted to the crowd. "You'll be sorry." Deputy Todd led the mayor to the door and shared some harsh, but private words the rest of us couldn't hear. My guess is Deputy Todd was more than willing to arrest the mayor but showed more restraint than I thought possible, instead leaving him with a stern warning instead.

Harper stepped up onto the counter to address the crowd. "Is that who we want as our mayor? A man who threatens and insults us? Our little Mayor Dewey has always been there when we needed him—always been there for support, to lend a paw or give a cuddle. Now it's time to support him. I ask you all, will you vote for Dewey?"

The diner erupted in cheers, so much so that I had to cover my ears. Harper had them in a frenzy, with a little help from Mayor Jim, no doubt. She hopped off her perch and skipped over to Angie and me.

"Did you hear all that?" she asked gleefully. "It couldn't have gone better if I'd scripted it. Mayor Jim played right into my hands. Dewey's a shoo-in for sure."

"I hope the mayor's all right," asked Angie. "He seemed pretty upset."

Harper scoffed. "He'll be fine. He just needs to cool off. His perfect entitled world ripping apart, and he's finally having to struggle for once. Boo hoo."

"When is the debate?" I asked. "And how will Dewey be able to debate Mayor Jim if he can't talk?"

"The debate is on Tuesday, election on Thursday. And don't worry about Mayor Dewey. He may not have to say anything. After Mayor Jim's performance tonight, Dewey just has to sit back and wait for him to implode."

"Sounds like it will be an exciting night."

"Oh, it will be," said Harper. "Just you wait."

Thirteen

✧✧

"WOULD YOU POUR me another cup of coffee?" I asked Angie, holding out my mug for her to fill. We'd stopped at the bakery the next morning after church for cinnamon rolls and caffeine. We called Harper once church was out and told her to head over. The jail's visiting hours weren't until ten o'clock, so we had some time to kill before Angie and I would drive to Vista.

"Nice sermon from Pastor Basil, don't you think? I especially liked the part about imagining yourself as a clod of dirt."

"Mm-hmm," I mumbled, taking a sip. Pastor Basil's sermons were always a little odd, just like him.

"So, I imagined myself as a clod of dirt, right there in church. He said we should use our nutrients to help those around us. It was... interesting."

"That's a good word for it."

"And some people are loamier, and others are more like clay. And those who were clay should work on being loamier and those who were loamy should work on adding more clay to the mixture."

"You're definitely loamy, Angie. You give, give, give and maybe you should work on taking a little sometimes instead." I took another sip of coffee. "So you don't deplete all your nutrients."

Angie nodded. "I think that's exactly what Pastor Basil meant too. Do you want another cinnamon roll?"

"Sure, thanks."

"Have you read the *Vista View* article about the party yet?" she asked, handing me a rolled newspaper.

"I haven't had a chance." I scanned the front page for the article and finally found it in the bottom corner.

Town Smitten with Political Kitten

Dewey the cat has made his mark on Starry Cove. The longtime resident tomcat and his human handler, Harper Tillman, are sweeping the political stage by storm, ushering in a new challenge for incumbent Jim Thornen.

At a rally held Saturday night in Dewey's name, the town proved its support by showing up in droves to partake in the snacks, drinks, and party tricks. One trick they didn't anticipate was Mayor Thornen's unexpected arrival and outburst, claiming the residents were "going to regret this" before being ushered out the doors by local Deputy Sheriff Todd Newman. This eruption could prove costly for

> Mayor Thornen, who trails in the polls by ten points going into Tuesday's debate.

"I see you're reading the article," said Harper, striding into the bakery. "Went pretty well, I'd say. The polls put Dewey up by ten points."

Angie huffed. "Those polls aren't scientific."

"It's a small town, Angie, and everyone was at the party last night."

"Not everyone," I said. "A few people were missing."

"But only a few." Harper grabbed the cinnamon roll Angie had placed on the countertop. "What time are you two going to Vista?"

"The jail opens in thirty minutes, so we'll leave soon."

"Blister will be glad to see us," said Angie. "So at least he knows people are fighting for him."

"And I still haven't been able to track down those two slippery twins, Dustin and Justin."

"They're probably trying to hide, which sounds pretty suspicious to me."

"To me too, but until I'm able to talk to them, we won't know what they're guilty of, if anything."

We were finishing our cinnamon rolls when Angie's phone rang. "Hello?" she answered. "Yes, this is Angela Owens." Harper and I waited for the call to end, only catching Angie's side of the conversation. "Today?" Angie asked, surprised. "I thought it was next Sunday. No, no, it's okay. Today will be fine—ten o'clock." She hung up, face drained.

"Who was that?" I asked. "You look like you're in shock."

"Remember that article I told you about?"

"Yeah."

"Well, the interview is today—here, in about fifteen minutes. I must have confused it with next Sunday on my calendar." She shook her head, irritated at her own absentmindedness. "At least I'm dressed for church and not covered in flour."

"Don't worry. I'll still go see Blister. You can visit him tomorrow."

"Thanks Poppy. This article is really important for the bakery."

"And we need to get out of your way," said Harper, shoving the last bit of cinnamon roll in her mouth.

"I'll see you both tonight," I said.

"Oh, yes," Angie said, excitedly. "I do love our girls' night tradition. See you both then."

***

Visiting hours were short on Sunday—just two hours—so I wanted to be sure to arrive at ten when the jail opened to visiting friends and family. I'd never been to the Vista jail before, but it was right next to the county office building, which I knew well, so it wasn't hard to find. In fact, the two buildings looked quite similar—gray marble, steps up to an entrance, few windows, if any. Yep, it was a regular government building for sure.

A security guard manned the counter inside the jail, and he handed me a form to complete before I could visit any inmate. Thankfully, Vista wasn't exactly a hub of crime, so there wasn't much demand for visiting hours today.

After completing my form, the guard escorted me behind the barred doors and into a small room with seating stations separated by plexiglass, just like in the movies. I spotted Blister sitting at the first plexiglass station. He waved enthusiastically as I sat down and picked up the line to talk to him through the glass.

"Hi Poppy," he said. "This is a surprise. I wasn't expecting any visitors."

"Angie would have come too but something urgent came up. She said she'll be by soon enough, though."

"Aw, poor Angie. This is probably pretty hard on her."

"And it's not hard on you?"

"Well, sure. But I didn't do anything, so what do I have to worry about?"

"Blister, Deputy Todd is convinced you're guilty. This is serious."

"What can I do, though?" He looked around the small room. "I'm locked in here."

"I know, sorry. I'm doing everything I can to get you out. I've got some leads going, but I have a few questions still."

"Ask me anything. What do I have to lose?"

I didn't expect Blister to be averse to my questions, but I was expecting a little more fire from him—a little more grit. He seemed defeated and ready to just let whatever happened happen. Being innocent in his own mind isn't enough to get him acquitted in a court of law.

"You said you went to the hardware store after everyone left the house. Was there anyone else in there that you remember?"

"I don't remember seeing anyone other than Trevor," he said. "Trevor should remember me. Hasn't he said so?"

"Trevor is somewhere deep in the jungles of Costa Rica right now, so he's not confirming anyone's alibi. It's up to you to remember if someone else was there."

Blister frowned. "I didn't see anyone, but I may have heard some noise in the back rows, against the wall. I never saw him. Or her, I guess. It's hard to say, you know—I was just there to pick up a few items and never thought it would be important to remember."

"But you think someone was there in the hardware store with you and Trevor?"

"Yeah, I think so."

This confirmed what Ursula said before, but it didn't help that neither of them saw the other.

"What about Dustin and Justin? What's their story?"

"The twins? Well, they're hard workers. Bicker a lot, but that's part and parcel for a demolition crew."

"Do you know where I could find them? They may have information that could help get you out of here."

"I remember them mentioning they liked to go to that casino—the one just out on the reservation. They're big gamblers, I think."

"Fantasy sports, perhaps?" I asked.

"Yeah. Among other things."

"There's one more thing I have to ask, Blister, and this is hard for me." I steeled myself before asking, "Did you ever say you'd kill Edgar Biggs?"

"What? No, I could never kill anyone." He shook his head.

"But did you *say* it? Dimitri claimed you were so

mad at one point you said you'd kill him."

"Oh, that." His eyes cast down and his shoulders slumped. "But I didn't mean it."

"What was it about?"

"Well, Quentin mentioned in private that Edgar was going to start his own business—competing business. I was pretty mad 'cause I'd been employing him for years and thought it was an underhanded thing to do."

"And Dimitri heard you say you'd kill him?"

"I may have said it, but it was just an outburst, nothing behind it."

"This is tough, Blister. Unless I can find someone who can swear you weren't at the house when Edgar was murdered, it isn't looking too good."

"What do you think I should do?"

I shrugged, overwhelmed with the facts. "Call a lawyer."

***

I parked my Prius in the small casino parking lot a few miles outside of Vista on the reservation. Sunday was clearly a day to gamble, as the lot was almost full, and I had to do a few loops before I found a spot. It was the middle of the day, but the full marquee and blue and green neon lights blazed even now advertising their keno game and players' odds on the penny slots.

As soon as I walked through the door, my nose filled with the scents of stale beer and potato chips. The clang of a hundred slot machines filled the large space and a hazy room in the far back, walled off in glass, was obviously the smokers' area. It would take a miracle for me to find Dustin and Justin here—assuming they were here at all.

I'm not sure why, but I couldn't imagine the twins spending their time playing slots. They seemed more like table or card players to me—higher stakes, bigger money. The table games were stationed in the center of the main casino floor, with the slot machines rounding out the edges to lure the smaller spenders inside. I sat at one of the slot machines at this border to the card tables and put a dollar into the feeder. My credits popped up and I pulled the lever. Nothing, of course. I was just trying to blend in, not really playing, so my eyes scanned the tables as I pulled the lever again.

Two heads, close together and very much alike, sat at one of the blackjack tables lined up to the left of center. Bingo. I was pretty sure these heads belonged to my targets. I pulled the lever once more and stood up, ready to head their way.

Bells and lights flashed at my machine as the credits total soared. I guess I'd won something. I looked around at the faces nearby, but most people were engrossed in their own machines, slowly wasting away their savings trying to strike it rich. I quickly cashed out my winnings and walked away before I got sucked in.

"Hello there," I said cheerfully and sat down at the card table next to the twins. They stared at me blankly, obviously surprised to see me at a casino in the middle of a day on a Sunday.

The dealer eyed me up and down and saw that I carried no chips. "You have to play if you want to sit at the table."

"Oh." I hopped back up. "I just wanted to talk to my friends here."

"You can get chips at the station against the wall." She pointed back toward the entrance.

"Cards really aren't my thing." I turned back to Dustin and Justin. "Can I buy you two some drinks?"

They exchanged looks, then checked their chip stacks, which were running low.

"Sure," said one of them. He had slightly longer hair and wore a green T-shirt. Or maybe it was a trick of the low lighting. "Thanks Poppy."

I guided them over to a nearby bar and took a seat at an empty table. A server came around and took our drink orders then disappeared as quickly as she'd arrived.

"What are you doing here?" asked the one with shorter hair, who wore a blue shirt with splatters of paint on the front.

I shook my head. "I'm sorry, but which one are you?"

"I'm Justin."

"And I'm Dustin," said the one in the green T-shirt with longer hair.

"I was hoping I could ask you both some questions about Edgar's death. First, I'm really sorry. I'm not sure if you knew him well, but it's still sad."

"We're not too broken up about it, but thanks."

"Yeah," said Justin. "We're okay. Probably tough for his kids. Our dad died when we were young too."

"Oh, I'm sorry."

The server reappeared with our drinks and handed them out.

"Can you tell me what you two did once Blister shut down for the day? I know it was raining pretty hard and you two were stuck outside."

"We packed up and left, that's all," said Dustin. "I

hate working in the rain and mud."

"Yeah, we always get stuck outside when everyone else gets to work where its dry. We finished chucking the pile of demo into the dumpster then took off."

I took a sip of my drink, trying to act casual. "And did you see anyone else when you were leaving?"

They looked at each other, then Justin asked, "What's with all the questions?"

"Sorry about that, I'm just eager to get my renovation going again. You know they shut down the project because of the investigation. The sooner its solved, the sooner we can all get back to work." So far, this excuse had seemed plausible to the others, and I was hoping it would work on the twins as well.

They exchanged a long look, as though speaking telepathically.

"I think we said goodbye to Maisie. She was just inside the side door into the kitchen. Blister wouldn't let us any further into the house on account of our muddy boots, so we didn't see anyone else."

Dustin scoffed. "He said we were filthy and muddy. What's he expect when he makes us work in the rain for hours?"

"Someone mentioned to me that you had a fight with Edgar. What was that about?"

"Everyone fought with Edgar," said Justin.

"And Edgar liked to pick fights," added Dustin.

This was certainly not the first time I'd heard that Edgar was a bully, and it was hard to discount what they were saying since it seemed a universal truth.

"A few people have mentioned that you owe them money too. Something about a fantasy sports league, I think it was."

They didn't exchange glances this time. They both just stared straight at me.

"Did you owe Edgar money?"

"No ma'am," said Justin smoothly. "We didn't owe Edgar any money."

"Do you play in any fantasy leagues?" Dustin asked me. "We have a few slots in ours if you're interested."

"No thanks. I'm not really a sports person. I've only just started watching baseball."

I sat back with my drink trying to act casual during the awkward standoff between us. They knew I was digging, and I knew they were hiding something. Unfortunately, Dustin and Justin were each other's alibis, which would be a tough nut to crack, and Maisie said she *may* have seen them leave that day.

"Have you talked to Maisie yet?" asked Justin, as though he'd read my mind. "She was Edgar's ex-wife, in case you didn't know."

"I did know, thanks. And she said she wants the hundred dollars you owe her."

Dustin and Justin scowled.

"What about Cho?" asked Dustin. "She seemed really eager to get onto your project. When we told her about the job and that Edgar would be on the crew, she immediately asked us to hook her up with Blister. That's how she got on."

"Really? You told her about the job?"

"That's right. We run in similar circles, most of us."

This was news to me, especially since Cho said she barely knew these two.

Dustin looked down at his glass. "You got anymore

questions for us? My drink's empty."

"No, but thanks for your time guys." Perhaps I had no more questions for right that moment, but maybe later. If these guys didn't owe Edgar money, what motive would they have had? This wasn't helping me get any closer to freeing Blister. I headed reluctantly out of the casino with my winnings. I'd really hoped finally getting a hold of these two would answer some looming questions, but it seemed more like a wash.

I shoved my purse into the car and wound my way through the parking lot and out onto the road. As I turned onto the street, I saw a woman seated at the bus stop, gray hair flowing wildly, staring straight at me with bugged eyes. Greta. *What is she doing here?* I had a sinking suspicion that she'd been following me this whole time. This woman was creeping me out. What else had she seen? What did she know?

Fourteen

It was a beautiful evening, cool and crisp. From the porch I could hear the waves crashing at the bottom of the cliff, steady and regular like a heartbeat. I waited there for Angie and Harper to arrive, as we'd previously planned, to continue discussing our next steps regarding the notebook and what we'd found.

Mayor Dewey had already joined me and now sat lazily in my lap, a patch of warmth to cut the coolness of the air, and I didn't dare disturb him. He seemed unperturbed by the previous night's festivities and excitement, probably because he spent most of his time sleeping in one of the diner's booths.

Angie appeared in the fading light, making her way from her cottage down the street, cutting across the roundabout. There was no traffic this time of night—honestly, any night—so she walked freely from across the road and up to the house.

"Hi Angie," I said as she came up the steps. "How'd the interview go?"

"Oh my gosh, Poppy, it was amazing." She plopped herself down on the bench next to me. "They wanted to know about the bakery and how I got started in baking. Roy hung back, of course, even though he's a big part of the bakery's success too. And then they took pictures and everything. I had hoped to make a few of my best pies for the photos—some real show-stoppers—but since they caught me off guard, I had to make do with the standard pies that were already in the case." She shook her head at the lost opportunity.

"I'm sure they were beautiful."

"Thanks, but those hi-definition lenses will pick up every imperfection."

I was sure the article and Angie would be a hit. She was always extra hard on herself and self-deprecating to a fault. "I can't wait to read it when it comes out."

"It won't be out for a few months at least—probably their winter edition—but I'm sure it will kick up business, so it's a good thing we're bringing on staff. Anyway, enough about me. How was Blister?"

"I don't think he knows how serious his predicament is. He seemed almost resigned."

Angie's face fell. "Poor Blister. He's never been a fighter. He has a temper sometimes, but I'm sure he believes truth will win out."

"Not while Deputy Todd has his sights on him. Blister confirmed there was another person in the hardware store, but he doesn't know who, which lands us exactly where we were before—no solid alibi."

Harper interrupted our gloomy mood with a holler from the street. Her mood couldn't have been brighter.

"Hey there, what's wrong?" she asked, walking up

on Angie and I lamenting Blister's situation.

"We still have nothing that helps Blister," said Angie.

"He didn't have anything to add today?"

"Not really," I said. "At least not anything that would outright free him."

Harper tapped her chin. "I've been thinking about that since last night. My mind's been so focused on Mayor Dewey's campaign that I haven't had much time to think about anything else."

"And?" I asked, urging her to continue.

"Remember when you got up and asked everyone there if they'd been in the hardware store?"

"Yes, but none of them were. That doesn't really help us."

"But it does. We know every person in town who was there, which means we can figure out everyone in town who *wasn't* there to answer your question."

Angie's face brightened. "And one of *them* could very well be Blister's alibi. We just need to track them down."

"Okay, who wasn't there?" I asked. "I don't remember seeing Nick Christos, do either of you?"

Angie shook her head. "No, and Trevor wasn't there. But I guess that makes sense."

"No Kenny Trotter either. What about him?"

"Bea mentioned to me that he rarely comes to town anymore, ever since, you know…"

"Right." Harper nodded. "I know very well. Anyone else?"

We sat in silence for another minute, wracking our brains going over the party in our minds. I shook my head.

"I can't think of anyone else that I haven't already asked."

"You should question Nick then," said Angie, turning to me eagerly. "As a handyman, he's likely to have been at the hardware store that day."

"I'll talk to Nick first thing in the morning."

"Why not now?" Angie wailed. "Blister's spending another night in jail."

I shook my head. "Because even if Nick has something to share, Deputy Todd won't be too happy if I wake him up in the middle of the night or disturb him during his favorite television show. He'd be more inclined to blow me off completely. We have to play it cool."

Angie sat back on the bench and crossed her arms, knowing I was right, even if she didn't like it. We had a lead, and that's what was important.

"And if Nick doesn't pan out, we're still left with nothing. I found Dustin and Justin at the casino today, but they shared very little—just pointed me back toward Maisie as Edgar's ex-wife."

"That's nothing new," said Harper. "She's got plenty of motive baked in."

"And they mentioned that Cho was really interested in working on the project. So much so that she asked them to introduce her to Blister."

"So what?" asked Harper.

I shrugged. "Nothing, really. It's just that when I talked to Cho, she made it seem like she barely knew the twins. And something else weird happened when I left the casino. I spotted Greta at the bus stop outside, and she was staring right at me."

"Creepy." Harper scrunched her face. "What a

weirdo."

"Was she following you?"

"I have to assume so. It was too great a coincidence since the casino is way out on the reservation. I'm afraid she's been tracking me."

Angie looked around at the foliage bordering the property, some which grew near enough to the porch for someone to eavesdrop. "We should go inside then. What if she's in the bushes right now?"

We quickly moved inside the mansion and took up seats in the living room on the dusty sofa. I pulled out the book we'd found in the basement and opened to a page I'd tabbed for reference. "I had some time today to go through the book. This chapter is about old railways in the area. Since there was a big logging industry around here, they needed the railroads to take the lumber out for processing and distribution."

"I only know of the Amtrak that runs through Vista," said Angie. "Are there more?"

"These probably don't exist anymore—or at least they're not in use."

"There are definitely old tracks around here," said Harper. "I've seen them. Some are deep in the woods. You can kind of see the route because the trees growing up around them are all young compared to the big redwoods."

"Oh," said Angie. "You're right. There are some old rail ties off the side of the Coastal Road. But what does this have to do with the notebook?"

"Remember what we read?" I pulled the picture up on my phone. "The note scribbled here reads 'Find P byway the line.' I'm wondering if that means a rail line."

"It's possible." Harper turned the photo in my hand her way to get a better look. "What's P then?"

"I hadn't gotten that far." Honestly, I was expecting them to be more excited about the railroad connection than they were. Maybe it wasn't as strong a connection as I thought. After all, "line" could mean a lot of things—latitude, longitude, that type of thing.

Angie and Harper drifted off in discussion about Angie's upcoming hire and Dewey's upcoming debate against Mayor Jim. I flipped through the book again, hoping something would jump out at me, but I didn't know the area well enough to have a clue. I turned to the chapter on towns and settlements, which went into great detail about the shanty towns and more prosperous villages that popped up during the lumber boom. There was a mention of a town call Prosperity, which was one of the larger logging villages and the book mentioned it ran along a railway.

"Do either of you know where Prosperity is?"

"Never heard of it," said Harper.

"What is it?" asked Angie.

"I don't know, some town that's mentioned in Slatherby's book. I'm trying to find our P."

"What if P is actually a person?" asked Harper. "It just says, 'find P.'"

Angie stared up at me curiously. "Or it could mean a pond. Maybe we have to find a pond?"

I tossed the book aside and grabbed a handful of the snack mix Harper had brought. That P could stand for anything at this point and the search felt futile. Worse, the only person who may know what it meant was Greta, and I was loath to bring her in after day-stalking me for who knows how long. I'd have to take some time at the library in Vista if I wanted to learn more. I just had to watch my back.

Fifteen

EARLY THE NEXT morning I was on the hunt. I searched for Nick at his house first, which seemed like the logical starting point, but when that proved a dead end, I decided to just call him instead. The line rang a few times but went to voicemail. I left my info and asked him to call me back, but that didn't stop my search.

While driving back into town I spotted Lovie and Deputy Todd walking along the sidewalk. Despite what she said, if anyone knew where everyone in town would be at any given moment, it was Lovie. My tires squealed as I braked to a halt and quickly got out of my car, running after them down the sidewalk.

I caught up to them all the way at the roundabout. "Lovie," I panted, finally reaching her.

"Poppy." She sounded surprised as she turned around to find me heaving from the jog. "What on earth are you doing?"

Once I caught my breath, I managed to ask, "Have you seen Nick Christos today?"

"Nick?" she wondered. "Yes, I saw him at the diner when I stopped in to talk to Shelby. I was waiting for Todd—I mean, the deputy."

Deputy Todd's eyes narrowed, and he hooked his thumbs into his belt loops. "What are you up to, Miss Lewis?"

"Something good, I hope. What are you doing now and where will you be later?"

Lovie beamed up at Deputy Todd. "We're going on a lovely walk then stopping at the bakery for Todd's—I mean, the deputy's—favorite donuts."

"If you're looking for me, I'll be in Vista at the station later. Why?"

"I might have a lead on Blister's alibi. Just be ready, okay?"

Deputy Todd grunted. "I told you to stay out of it, Miss Lewis. I don't want any more of your shenanigans."

"These aren't shenanigans, Deputy." I turned back toward the diner. "I promise."

I rushed down the sidewalk and across the street, past the bakery, and to the diner next door. I barreled through the door and quickly scanned the booths, searching for Nick's gorgeous face. Nothing. I was crestfallen. I'd just have to wait for him to call me back, which could take forever.

"Good morning, dearie," said Shelby, sidling up, her beehive wobbling with every step. "Here for some breakfast?"

"No, sorry Shelby. I was looking for Nick. You don't happen to know where he is, do you?"

Shelby smiled and looked down at the floor and gave a little kick. "Hey Nick, get up here. Poppy's looking for you."

"What?" He hauled himself out from under the counter and staring up at me, confused.

Finally, something was going my way.

"Oh, hi Poppy." He brushed a lock of his golden hair out of his sun-kissed face. Nick was the town's resident Greek god, chiseled from fine stone with the power to woo any woman who crossed his path. It was always a bit jarring talking to Nick, and I always felt like I needed to avert my eyes so I didn't simply stare at him and turn to goo.

"I'm so glad I found you," I said, staring just past his ear. This was a trick Angie taught me—one she used with Nick as well.

"I'm sorry I missed Harper's party last night. I had other plans, but I really wish I could have been here. Lovie said it was great. Shelby asked me to come over this morning to fix some things that broke last night."

I grimaced at Shelby and whispered, "I'm sorry." She shrugged it off, shook her head, and stared down at Nick the way I said I typically try to avoid, satisfied grin on her face.

"Nick, I have a very important question to ask you."

"Okay," he responded slowly.

"Can you remember where you were last Tuesday around lunchtime?"

"Tuesday around lunchtime..." he repeated. "I'm not sure. That's almost a whole week ago."

"Do you remember going to the hardware store?"

He scratched his head and looked uncertain. "Yeah, I think so."

"You think so, or you *know* so?" I asked.

He nodded slowly. "I know so. I had to pick up some wooden stakes, but I dropped the box of them and had to pick them all up off the floor."

"Are the stakes located in the back by the wall?"

"Yeah, how did you know? I didn't think you were there that often."

It *was* him. Nick was the one Ursula and Blister both heard in the store that day. He was my best chance.

"Nick," I said in a clear and steady voice. "Do you remember seeing anyone else in the hardware store while you were there?"

"Well, Trevor was there behind the counter."

"Anyone else? Anyone at all?"

"I think I remember hearing Ursula's voice, but she was only there for a minute and I had already dropped the stakes and was picking them up."

"Anyone else?" I asked hopefully.

"Well, let me think. I messed those stakes up pretty bad, so I sat on the floor to get them back in the box the way they'd come. It was like a puzzle, those sticks in that box."

I was losing my patience, but I let him continue, hoping that talking it out would get him to remember.

"Then, I think about the time I was done another person came in."

"Who?" I demanded.

Nick looked confused again. "I'm not sure. I didn't recognize his voice—I remember that."

"So, it wasn't someone from Starry Cove?"

"Probably not—I'd say I know most folks here."

"And did you see this man? Did you get a look at him at all?"

"He was there for a long time. I was still puzzling out those stakes—did I mention how difficult they were to fit back in that box?"

"Yes, you did. What about the man?"

"Oh yeah. Well, by the time I got the stakes squared away and got up off the ground, the guy was already at the counter with Trevor."

"What did he look like?"

"Big guy, really tall. He wore a dark blue shirt, I think. Anyway, he and Trevor talked a good long while, but I don't know when he left since after I'd organized all those stakes, I also dropped a container of rubber bathtub plugs and had to clean those up, too. Can you believe it?"

"Would you say this guy was construction-y looking?"

"Yeah, most definitely. He had a million pockets on his pants."

I leaned over the counter and pulled Nick up by the scruff of his shirt. "Come with me," I demanded, trying to haul him over.

"I'm coming, I'm coming," he pleaded.

"Poppy, don't you steal my handyman." Shelby scurried after us. "You bring him back!" she yelled as I led Nick out of the diner.

I glanced into the window of the bakery next door and spotted Deputy Todd. He and Lovie hadn't made it out with their donuts yet.

"It's not Blister!" I yelled, pushing Nick through the door as it chimed.

Deputy Todd, startled from the shout, squeezed the donut he held carefully in his hands and the jelly filling squirted onto his uniform. "Confound it, Miss Lewis." He wiped the sugary red ooze off his badge.

Angie stood behind the counter, hopeful. "What do you mean, Poppy?"

"Nick saw him." I shoved Nick toward Deputy Todd. "Nick saw Blister at the hardware store—exactly when he said he was there."

Everyone looked at Nick, whose eyes bulged wide at the sight of the deputy staring him down.

I gave Nick a small poke. "Tell them."

He gulped before speaking. "I saw a big burly man in a blue shirt at the hardware store last Tuesday."

Deputy Todd eyed Nick slowly, then glanced my way. "She didn't tell you to say all this, did she?"

"No, sir," Nick responded quickly. "See, I was at the store around lunchtime looking for wooden stakes, but the box fell and—"

I broke in, "And he saw Blister. Big man, blue shirt. Nick said he looked like the guy was on a construction crew. C'mon, Deputy, you know it's Blister he saw."

Deputy Todd let out a heavy sigh. Angie stared at him hopefully. I held my breath. Lovie drank in the spectacle. "All right," he said finally. "If Nick here swears he saw Blister at the hardware store, then I guess Blister was at the hardware store."

"I swear it," said Nick, terrified he'd somehow be in trouble.

Angie burst into tears. "Oh Poppy, you did it," she wailed as she hugged me tightly around the waist and stomped her little feet. "We're going to free Blister!"

***

My car tires squealed as I jerked to a stop in a parking

spot in front of the jail. Angie joined me a short time later in her own car and we waited impatiently on the steps for Deputy Todd to arrive. He took his sweet time, but finally drove up and parked his truck and Angie and I rushed in.

Deputy Todd strode up to the guard stationed at the counter behind the bulletproof glass. He leaned in and whispered something through a small microphone.

"Hauser, sir?" the man asked, his voice filling the small lobby through the speaker. He looked at me and Angie, clearly confused at this sudden request.

Deputy Todd put his hands on his hips. "You heard me, Ramirez. Hauser, pronto."

The guard, Ramirez, quickly slid Deputy Todd a sheet of paper and a pen through the slot in the glass and the deputy scribbled his name and passed it back.

"Grab his things and bring him out," Deputy Todd said through the microphone.

"Yes, sir." Ramirez headed behind a heavy locked door to an area behind the scenes. A few moments later, the officer reappeared at the lobby door leading Blister, who towered above him. Blister clutched a small bag in his hand, weighed down with his personal belongings—wallet, tape measure, pencils, that sort of thing.

"Angie, Poppy—what's happening?" He rushed over to us, smiling. He gave Angie a big hug. "The guard said I was free to go."

"That's right, Blister," said Angie. Her neck bent severely as she stared up at the gigantic man. "Poppy's figured out who saw you in the hardware store, so we know you didn't kill Edgar."

"That's great news, but did you find out who did?" He turned to Deputy Todd, who looked startled at this expectation that he actually solve the case.

"We're, uh, still reviewing the evidence."

I crossed my arms and looked at the deputy doubtfully. "And are you any closer? I'm glad that Blister is free, and I'd like to start on my renovations again—without a killer on the loose."

"There are leads, Miss Lewis, that I am not privy to discuss."

"And my renovations?"

He waved a dismissive hand. "Fine. You can continue with your project. But the house remains open to investigation if I request it."

A satisfied grin crossed my face. "Excellent. Blister," I said, turning to the big man, "when can you start again?"

His shoulders slumped and Angie propped him up as much as her little body could. "I'd appreciate a good night's sleep in my own bed. And I'll have to contact the crew, but I can be there tomorrow morning, ready to work."

"That'd be great." Having Blister back would get the project rolling again. And even if someone on the crew did murder Edgar, with Blister around, I felt safe enough to continue my questioning and unravel the threads.

***

It was midday when I arrived at the Vista library just down the street from the jail and county office building. I'd brought Slatherby's book with me and stowed it securely in my backpack as I got out of the car. My eyes did a quick scan around the parking lot and surrounding streets, searching for Greta, but there was no sign of the diminutive woman.

I started first with the young librarian behind the reference counter. "Hi there," I said. "I'm hoping you can help me find anything about a local town called Prosperity."

The librarian tapped the side of her glasses, thinking, but eventually shook her head. "Doesn't ring a bell. But you could go through our newspaper and microfiche collection."

I cringed. Slogging through heaps of records sounded too laborious for the time I had at my disposal. "I was hoping to avoid that. I could be here forever."

"Actually, we've digitized the records, so you can search them for specific keywords."

That was a relief. "In that case, where do I start?"

"At the computers." She pointed to two rows of computer cubbies lined up along the back wall.

I entered the password for the database and was soon browsing through old copies of the *Vista View* newspaper. The copies went back to 1895, when the newspaper was founded, but I wanted to search anyway for any mention of Prosperity. The system wasn't infallible, the librarian had warned me, and if I was really determined, I would probably have to search the records manually. Let's see, that meant visually scanning well over a hundred years' worth of newspapers—published daily—for the slight mention of a town name. I kept my fingers crossed that the digital search would bring back a hit.

First, I searched by keyword in article titles, then keywords anywhere within the text. Nothing. I pulled out the book and checked to make sure I was spelling the town name correctly, but I was, so that wasn't the problem. Next, I tried searching for articles about old logging communities. That turned up a few results, but not what I was looking for, so I tried to find information about the railroad lines that ran through the area. I finally got a good hit in one of the earliest *Vista View* editions.

As I scanned the article, I learned that many of the logging rail lines that had previously run through the large forested areas shut down due to changes in logging regulations and laws. The rails must have then fallen into disrepair, the forests reclaiming them and hiding them from the human eye. It wouldn't have taken long, either, in these redwood forests. The ferns would grow quickly, covering the metal rails and the ties would quickly break down in the moist conditions. The article gave little detail on the location of the rail lines and included no map. Harper and Angie's knowledge of one of these old lines was the only location we had to go on.

I also used my time and access to the database to search for information on Claude Goodwin, the builder and first owner of the mansion. Everything I found was consistent. Claude Goodwin made his money in the logging industry and built the Victorian as a testament to his fortune.

Although there were fewer mentions, Atticus Goodwin proved to be a much more interesting fellow. There were no *Vista View* articles about him—he was already a distant memory by then—but I did find a scholarly paper about piracy on the west coast in the early days of the United States, before most of the western states were even states.

Atticus Goodwin came across as a mysterious figure and one of the most prolific pirates of the late eighteenth century. But what caught my eye was the mention of a rumored pirate enclave located deep in the forest by the name of Prosper Hollow, which sounded to me an awful lot like Prosperity. Primary sources for the paper included a missionary's journal and record of oral traditions of the local native tribes. I guess when you went back that far, written sources were scarce—there were no libraries or registrars' offices around here in those days. Still, this was a tough coincidence to dismiss. I made a note on the sheet of scratch paper provided by the library and shoved it securely into Slatherby's book.

I thanked the librarian as I exited the building. Safely in my car, I called Harper and Angie and asked if they were available later to do a little reconnaissance on the information I'd gathered.

"I'll be available once the bakery closes at three today."

"That's perfect. We'll have enough light to search around, and I'll bring flashlights just in case."

Harper's schedule was a bit spottier. "I've taken some time off work to prepare for the debate, which is tomorrow, I'll remind you."

"I know, but this could lead us to those gold doubloons you're so eager to find."

"I'm not silly enough to think we'll find real gold doubloons. Dewey and I are working on his debate prep, but I can be over after that—maybe three o'clock, okay?"

Perfect, I thought. We'll have plenty of time to snoop around. "Great. I'll see you then."

Sixteen

I WAITED ON the porch for Angie and Harper to both arrive. My backpack weighed heavily on my shoulders, laden with flashlights and Slatherby's book, for reference, and I had my phone charged so I could easily refer to the pictures of Arthur and Greta's notebook if we needed them.

I hadn't fallen off my guard, so I still scanned the street and bushes for Greta, wondering if she would be bold enough to hide under a shrub in order to get information. This seemed like a far-fetched possibility though, since Greta was so old and frail. She'd probably get stuck under a dense bush and her body wouldn't be found for months.

Angie rounded the corner, and I met her on the sidewalk under the arched trellis.

"Cupcake?" she asked, offering me a beautifully decorated pink cupcake.

"Sure. What's this from?"

"Leftovers from a custom birthday order. I've got

one for Harper too. Where is she?"

"She should be here soon. She was working on campaign stuff."

Angie shook her head. "That woman needs to get her head out of the clouds. I get that she's bent on ruining the mayor, and it's true that the mayor doesn't really do a lot, but I wish she'd run herself instead of Dewey."

"She seems pretty motivated, maybe she'll realize she has a taste for politics and consider it next time."

"Maybe," said Angie. "Look, there's her car."

We both waited as Harper parked her car and rushed up the sidewalk to the trellis. "I've been so busy with Dewey's campaign today, I forgot to ask how things went with Blister."

Angie beamed. "Oh, it went so well. Blister's out of jail and I took him home and got some warm food in him. Eventually, I had to get back to the bakery for this custom order—here, take this." Angie passed a cupcake to Harper. "Anyway, he's doing well."

"Thanks, and glad to hear about Blister. Does this mean you get to continue work on the house, Poppy?"

"Yes, finally." I rolled my eyes. "Deputy Todd deigned to grant me that one wish."

"So now that Blister is free and renovations are back on, what are we up to tonight?"

"I told you both on the phone that I found something at the library. Remember last night when we couldn't figure out what the P was in the scribble? I think it might be Prosper Hollow."

"Huh?"

Harper shook her head. "Didn't you ask us that last night?"

"No. I asked about Prosperity."

"Oh, well I still haven't heard of it," said Angie. "Why, is it important?"

"According to a paper I read, it was an old pirate enclave deep in the forest. Don't you think it's odd that the names are so similar?"

"Lots of names are similar, though," said Harper. "We have a Rambleton and Ramblerville nearby."

"I want to check out that old rail line you said you knew of in the woods. I want to follow it and see what we find. Slatherby's book said Prosperity was along a railway line."

"Bit of a coincidence for that place to be along the one railway that we know of, though, wouldn't it?"

I started counting off on my fingers. "A pirate town with a similar name starting with P, along a railway, near a place where Claude Goodwin, Atticus Goodwin's grandson, built one of the first mansions around that just happened to fall into the ownership of the man who wrote our notebook?" I held up my hand. "That's four threads that match up. I don't think it's too much of a leap."

"All right, let's check it out, but we need to head back before it gets too dark, so we've only got a few hours."

"I told Roy I'd be home by seven, and I don't want to be out in the woods in the dark either."

"We won't be out late. I'm meeting Ryan for dinner, anyway. But why are you two so reluctant? I thought you'd be more excited to figure this out."

Angie wrapped her little arm around me. "We are. It's just that we've got so much going on right now."

And I didn't. That was the unspoken end to Angie's words. She had her bakery's success to think about and was probably still floating on high from the magazine interview and Blister's freedom, and Mayor Dewey's campaign had completely hijacked Harper's attention. And I no longer had a house renovation to keep me occupied. All that would change tomorrow, though, once Blister and the crew were back.

"You're right," I said. "I've been so selfish, dragging you two off when you've got other priorities. Tomorrow, I'll be back working on the house, but tonight, would you humor me? I'd like to see where that rail line goes. It could be nothing, and the only thing we'll be out is a pleasant walk in the woods."

"Of course, Poppy," said Angie.

"I'm in, too. I really hope we find gold doubloons, though—Dewey's campaign hasn't been cheap."

***

My Prius glided smoothly on the paved Coastal Road as Harper navigated me toward the spot where the rail ties sat undisturbed. An opening appeared in the trees where a logging road led deeper into the forest and I turned off the main road to follow as it wound into the trees.

Harper squinted and leaned forward in her seat. "It's around here somewhere. I remember seeing it not too far off the Coastal Road. It juts out from this seasonal road."

"Usually, this path is closed in winter," said Angie. "We don't really get snow or anything, being this close to the coast, but the bad weather means no one is working in the forest. Plus, the mud alone can be dangerous."

After a bumpy ride on the unpaved dirt, Harper's arm shot out as she pointed to a spot just up ahead on the right. "There. That's it. You can see the trees are smaller."

There was no shoulder, so I parked the car in the middle of the road. We grabbed our things and inspected the site. The underbrush was still thick with ferns and other low-growing plants, as it is in most of the coastal redwood forests of California. I found a stick nearby and used it to move fronds out of the way, looking at the ground for signs of the rail tracks.

"Here." Angie waved us over. "This looks like one of the abandoned rail ties."

"And here's another," said Harper, just a few feet away.

Both were long since crumbled, but their distinctive shape still marked them as man-made. "This must be the spot then." I checked the road one last time, to make sure we hadn't been followed, but I saw no cars and no headlights. We truly were in the middle of nowhere out here, but I didn't trust that Greta hadn't shadowed us. "C'mon, let's head in."

It was easy to follow the path of the old rail line now, once a few of the deteriorating ties got us onto the track. Only occasionally did we stumble upon an actual rail. Most seemed to have long since been salvaged, but others remained in place, having rusted too much from the salty air.

Despite the mid-afternoon hour, the woods turned dark quickly. "Stay close," I warned.

"Where are those flashlights?" asked Angie.

I dug into my backpack and pulled out the three flashlights I'd brought and handed them out. They helped to steady our steps, but the way forward was obvious—the trees were simply missing—so we continued on deeper into the forest.

We'd meandered along the tracks for a quarter of an hour when Harper kicked a fern out of her path. "What are we even looking for?"

"Any sign of a town. Maybe an old abandoned building or something. It'll be old—over a hundred years, so there's probably not much left, if anything."

"What you're saying is, we're trying to find old decaying wood in an old decaying forest of wood?"

"That's about right, Harper," I said, losing my patience at her negativity.

"Great. Just wanted to be sure we weren't wasting our time or anything."

Angie shined her light at both of us. "Would you two stop?"

"I wasn't—" Harper tumbled to the forest floor. "Ouch, that hurt."

"What happened?" I asked, pulling her up to her feet.

"I tripped over something."

"Lots to trip over out here." I shined my flashlight at what had caused her to fall and saw that it was the rotting stump of an old post sticking up out of the ground, except it was broken, and only about four inches protruded from the earth—a perfect tripping hazard.

"What's that?" Angie pointed her flashlight to something laying on the ground nearby.

I shoved away decades of pine needles with my hands to uncover a metal sign. Its letters had faded almost completely, but upon the browned background, I could barely make out what it said: Prosperity.

"This is it," I said. "Prosperity."

We searched the immediate area with our flashlights, but saw nothing but trees, shrubs, and ferns.

Harper dropped the broken branch she'd been inspecting. "Not much here. Maybe a little further in?"

"What do we look for now, Poppy? Does anything in the notebook connect with this place?"

I pulled out my phone and we huddle around the glowing screen. Once I'd flipped to the map drawing, I zoomed in to the part about what I hoped was Prosperity. There were notations scribbled nearby, but none that we could decipher.

"I can't tell what anything is," said Angie.

"Me neither." My shoulders sagged. I looked back up toward the surrounding forest, but as the daylight faded it was becoming too hard to see very far. For all I knew, there could be the foundation of a building right in front of me, but with the overgrowth and low light, I'd never be able to tell.

"Did you hear that?" Angie shone her light back into the forest. "I thought I heard something behind us."

"Hear what?" Harper's flashlight scrambled wildly among the trees, searching for whatever Angie had heard.

"Not sure exactly. A twig snapping, I guess."

We turned back to the screen, zooming in on different areas of the map, looking for any clue. Suddenly, a loud crack echoed through the forest and splinters erupted from the tree next to my head.

"What the—" Another crack and more shards of bark flew as the three of us dove to the ground and under the cover of the shrubs and ferns.

"Someone is shooting at us," Harper whispered in haste. "Quick, turn off your lights."

We turned off our flashlights and I turned off my phone so even the faint glow wouldn't show through the darkening woods. Angie whimpered softly and clung to my arm. Her eyes were shut tight, wishing the danger away.

"It must be Greta," I whispered. "She's followed us here. It didn't sound too close and both shots missed."

"What do we do?" asked Harper.

I took in our surroundings. The rail line continued farther into the forest, heading north, and also led back to the logging road to the south. "She can't shoot at all of us at the same time," I said. "I'll create a distraction by running one way, and you two head to the car once I've got her attention."

Angie clutched my sleeve. "Poppy, no. You could get hurt."

"I'm fast. Harper, here, take my bag." I peeled myself out of the backpack straps as quietly as I could. "The car keys are inside the top pocket."

Harper gripped the straps. "Got it," she said, looking me straight in the eye and nodding. "We run for the car."

After a moment of thought, I handed her my cell phone. "Better take this too. It has the notebook pictures."

"What about you?"

Another shot rang out and hit a tree farther to the left of where we hid. The shooter must not be sure where we were hiding—or they were a terrible shot.

"I'll circle around and try to meet you on the road. But don't wait for me if you get shot at. We can't let anyone get ahold of Slatherby's book or the pictures."

Harper nodded, but Angie pinched her eyes shut and shook her head. "I'm a terrible runner and I'm going to die."

"You'll be fine, Angie. I have faith in you."

"I'll carry you if I have to," said Harper. "Just try to keep up and we'll be okay."

I leveraged myself up onto my hands, ready to lift up and make a break for it into the woods. Drawing a deep breath, I took off, following the old track line north and farther into the woods.

A shot fired from deep in the forest and a redwood bough behind me shuddered as a bullet flew through it. She was on to me. I ran as fast as I could, trying not to trip on anymore rotting posts or ties. Glancing back, I couldn't see Harper or Angie—I saw nothing but a brown and green blur of trees in the fading light.

I ran farther, planning on taking a hard left and circling back to the logging road to hopefully meet back up with Harper and Angie in our hybrid getaway car. Once I felt sufficiently far from my friends, I took the sharp turn into denser forest. I had to slow down as I waded through the denser brush, falling a few times onto my hands and knees, but I tried to follow parallel to the tracks so I wouldn't lose my way. Rustling shrubs about thirty yards behind me meant the shooter had also diverged off the track line. The rustling didn't come any closer though, and I assumed the shooter must think I'd simply hidden off the side of the railway nearby.

I slowed my pace, moving from tree to tree in near darkness, trying not to disturb any dead twigs or crispy fern fronds that might give away my position.

When I felt far enough away, I quickly angled back toward the tracks to the easier path and sprinted toward the logging road. It was almost fully dark now, and as I ran recklessly along the track, a sharp tree branch scratched my face. I put a hand up to my cheek and saw blood on my fingers but didn't stop running.

A few moments after I'd reappeared on the open path, so too did my pursuer. A bullet whizzed by and I covered my head with my hands, as though that would protect me. My lungs burned as I dashed down the dangerous overgrown tracks and, after what seemed like forever, crashed through to the logging road. My car was idling twenty yards ahead. Harper had turned it around to face the direction we'd come in, ready for a quick getaway. I could see Angie pressed up against the backseat window staring at me with dread, urging me to run faster.

As I reached the car, I jumped into the passenger seat and Harper hit the gas. The car eased higher in miles per hour, but my electric Prius was no diesel truck or speedway coupe.

"She's behind us," Angie wailed from the backseat.

We heard a shot, but it didn't hit the car, at least that I could tell. We all instinctively ducked. By the time I looked back, all I could make out was an indistinct figure standing on the edge of the forest, watching as we drove away in the faded light.

"I'll tell you one thing," Harper said as the car rattled down the logging road. "That wasn't some little old lady sprinting through the woods firing shots at our heads."

"No," I said, silently wondering who it could have been. "It sure wasn't."

Seventeen

WE DROVE STRAIGHT back to the house and tumbled out of the car, tired, cut up, and bruised from running through the forest.

"Thank you for the lovely evening." Harper wiped bits of pine needles off her pants. "Let's *not* do it again."

"We should go to Deputy Todd," said Angie, looking back and forth at Harper and me for agreement. "That person was trying to kill us."

"Deputy Todd isn't going to help us," I said. "And he'd only confiscate Slatherby's book—and probably Arthur's notebook too."

"Who the heck was that person? They came out of nowhere."

"I don't know." I shook my head and a pine needle fell from my hair onto to the ground. "Oh no. I've got to get ready for dinner with Ryan."

"You're still going?" asked Angie. "I feel like we need to file a report or—"

"No reports. No Deputy Todd."

"All right, but I'm not going into those woods again. No more adventures. In fact, I'm going home to Roy. This has all been a bit much for me."

"I'm out too," said Harper. "I still need to finish up some things for the debate tomorrow night—if I can even focus after what just happened."

"Let's meet up here before the debate. I'll see you both tomorrow. And don't mention what happened tonight to anyone—we don't know who that was in the forest."

We went our separate ways, and I rushed into the house to get ready to meet Ryan for dinner and to see his new gazebo. I plucked a few more pine needles from my hair and washed and tended the bloody scrape on my cheek. No amount of make-up would disguise it as anything other than a nasty wound.

I arrived at Ryan's bungalow just after seven. The light was on inside, but before I could walk up the porch to the door, Ryan came around the side and greeted me in his warm Scottish accent. He wore his signature V-neck sweater—this one was lavender.

"Good evening," he said. "I've got everything set up around back. Come this way." He led me around the side gate and into the backyard. As I rounded the house, a sea of string lights illuminated the yard. He'd wrapped them around the gazebo and up to the house, creating a soothing atmosphere, which was just what I needed after my near-death experience.

"It looks amazing. I can't believe you got all this set up."

"With a little help," he admitted.

"I'm glad you finally asked for it."

"Well, it was either that or have a pile of wood rotting in my backyard for the next decade."

"Good choice," I said, turning around to appreciate the lights.

"Wait, what's this?" He turned my head to the side with a gentle finger to get a better view of the cut on my cheek.

"It's just a minor scratch. Don't worry about it."

"That's not a minor scratch. You should come by the pharmacy tomorrow and I'll get you squared away."

"Thanks, but it's really nothing." I tried to change the subject, for both our sakes. I didn't want to think of earlier events either. "Show me the gazebo. I've been waiting to see it."

As we got closer to the finished structure, I could see a table inside with dinner already laid out. Ryan uncorked a bottle of red wine and filled two glasses. He raised his glass to mine and said, "To the completion of the longest gazebo construction project man has ever witnessed."

We clanked glasses and I took a sip, savoring the wine.

"Dinner awaits," he said, ushering me into the gazebo. Benches lined the sides, and we sat next to one another where he'd set up two plates.

"What's on the menu? And don't say burgers and chips."

"I wouldn't do that to you." He lifted the cover off a platter at the center of the table. "Spaghetti and meatballs from my favorite Italian restaurant in Vista—gourmet, mind you."

"Looks and smells amazing. One day when I have a kitchen again, I'll make you that dinner I've been threatening."

"And I can't wait." He filled our plates and we enjoyed the food, sharing small talk between bites.

After we'd eaten, Ryan popped inside to grab another bottle of wine. I took a moment to look at the beautiful gazebo under the twinkling lights. The atmosphere was so relaxing. This was a proper dinner, with good company, good food, and good wine. My mind drifted, possibly because of the wine. It was almost as if Ryan and I were—"

"—Motor Masters?"

"Sorry?" I asked. Ryan had returned from the house, but I'd clearly missed what he was saying.

"Did you hear about Motor Masters?" he repeated, stepping up into the gazebo.

"Oh, no, I haven't."

"Aye, seems like they're moving into the garage shop next to the bookstore. Glad to see a new business cropping up."

"You know, Arthur's got an old Vespa scooter. I wonder if I should get it fixed up?"

"*If* you should?" Ryan gaped. "Of course you should. I can picture you zipping around town on your scooter right now, smile on your face, wind blowing in your hair. Breathtaking."

We stared silently at one another for a moment. He'd called me breathtaking—well, he called the thought of me gallivanting on a Vespa scooter breathtaking, but that counts. Ryan set his glass down and placed a finger on my chin. My heart raced—from his touch—or the wine, I wasn't sure. He pulled me close and I closed my eyes.

Crack! My body shifted sideways and brought me

out of the moment. My eyes popped open as the wooden gazebo bench snapped and broke through the floorboards, Ryan and I tumbling along with it. My wine glass slipped from my hand as I fell and splashed onto Ryan's glasses.

I scrambled up from the rubble a moment later and winced when I saw a red stain on his face and sweater. "Ryan, I'm so sorry."

He stood up from the pile. "Oof, that was not pleasant. Are you all right?"

"I'm fine."

"Good." He wiped off his glasses and looked down on the broken section of the gazebo. The bench had completely split in two and the wooden boards making up the floor now hung from the support beam that poked out from the center support hub. He sighed. "That must have been the fifteen percent of it that I built."

***

While Ryan and I had a lovely dinner, the wrecked gazebo essentially ended the evening's festivities. But our conversation had left me with a task, and I intended to see it done, so the next morning I woke up early, deflated my air mattress and shoved it in the closet off the foyer. The renovation crew should be back today, or at least most of them, so I straightened up the rest of my temporary sleeping quarters and hid my dirty clothes.

Before anyone showed up, I took a stroll out to the shed behind the property, where Arthur had stowed away all sorts of junk, but also some treasures. One of those was the Vespa scooter I'd told Ryan about the night before.

I dug it out from behind the boxes of old newspapers

and magazines and brought it out into the morning light. At first glance, it needed a lot of work. I was no expert, but even I could tell it was pretty far gone. Sitting out in the shed in the salty coastal air hadn't done it any favors, but I could still make out the robin's egg blue paint color underneath some bits of rust and grime. If that Motor Masters place Ryan told me about was really going to open soon, maybe I'd take it in for restoration. But one project at a time. For now, I had the house to deal with, so I returned the scooter to the shed, covered it with a drop cloth I'd found inside, and left it there for the time being.

I spied Blister coming up the walkway as I returned to the house. "Hello there, Blister."

"Poppy, so glad to be back," he replied, as we met near the front porch steps. "I talked to a few of the others yesterday and had to leave a couple messages, but I hope most will be back on site by today."

"That's great news. Let's go inside and you can get resettled. I'll make some coffee."

The coffeemaker was still percolating when Maisie and Quentin arrived. The twins and Cho arrived a short time after that. I was wary of having a potential killer in the house, but Blister stood confidently next to me, and I didn't plan on being out of his sight. Everyone seemed pleased to be back on the job, though, and they got to work straight away as if they'd never left.

"No Dimitri," Blister said after the others had disbursed throughout the house. "I had to leave him a message yesterday, so maybe he missed it."

"Blister?" Quentin called out.

"Oh shoot, I forgot." Blister set down his coffee on a makeshift table. I followed him into the dining room where Quentin was cutting two-by-fours. "What do you need?"

"Can you check this cut for me? I was working on this when we, uh, left early the other day."

"Sure thing." Blister grabbed the wood and pulled out some sort of measuring device. "Shave a little more. This should be at forty-five degrees."

"Thanks," Quentin said, taking it back, then added for my clarification, "Blister's agreed to take on my apprenticeship now that Edgar's gone."

"It was the least I could do. I'm licensed, and I had no hesitation when he asked."

"That's kind of you. What do you have to do?"

"Oh, you know, watch over him. That sort of thing."

"I'm very close to my test," said Quentin. "It's not always easy finding someone who's willing to take on an apprentice, especially in such a rushed way, so I consider myself lucky. Thanks again, Blister."

Blister nodded. "No problem. No problem at all young man."

As Blister and I returned to our coffee, we ducked our heads into the living room. No Dimitri yet.

"I don't have time to hunt that man down."

"You should watch what you say now, Blister. Deputy Todd will jump on anything that gives him any reason to put you back in jail."

His face drained. "You're right. I didn't even think about that."

"You stay here with Quentin and don't worry about Dimitri. I know where to find him."

***

I parked my car in the near-empty gravel lot at the Vista Tavern. As I'd hoped, Dimitri's truck was also there. As I walked by the truck on my way into the bar, I noticed that the decal on the door was now damaged—defaced, really. It used to spell out "Dimitri's Drywall," but the words were scratched out in chaotic strokes, like someone had come by and scored the decal with their keys. I ran my hand over the scuff marks—they were deep, probably scraped the metal underneath.

At the door to the bar, I paused and closed my eyes for a few moments, trying to acclimate myself to the darkness I'd find inside the windowless room. As I walked in, Hank and Gus greeted me with lazy waves and a quick hello. Joe popped up from under the bar and gave me a holler as well.

"Pour me whatever you've got on tap," I said to Joe. "What, no game today?"

"It's a commercial," said Hank.

"Ahh, well in that case, has Dimitri been in?"

Three pairs of eyes shifted to a booth in the back.

"Gotcha." I nodded, taking the beer from Joe. "Thanks guys."

Dimitri rolled his eyes and took a large swig of beer as I came into view. "This lady," he muttered under his breath.

I plopped myself in the opposite bench in the booth. "Hi there."

"What you want now?" he asked in his thick accent. "I am trying to enjoy baseball game."

"Dodgers, eh?"

"Yeah. So what? You like Dodgers?" His words were already slurring. He must have started drinking early, and he'd probably had a few before I even showed up.

"No." I took a sip. "Hate 'em."

Dimitri lifted an eyebrow.

"I saw your truck outside. Pretty scratched up. What happened?"

At the mention of his truck, Dimitri dropped his gaze and stared at the table. "Nothing."

"Nothing happened? Rabid raccoons didn't do that to your car."

"I—" he started, "I have suspended license. Drywall license." He continued to stare at the table.

"You lost your license?"

"*Suspended*. It will be back soon, okay? I got mad and hurt truck, okay?"

"Okay. The authorities arrested Blister. Did you know that?"

"Blisser?" he asked, slurring badly now.

"That's right, but they've already let him go."

"So, they look for murderer?"

I nodded, taking another sip from my beer. I let him stew on that for just a minute. "Tell me where you were, Dimitri. You can clear your name."

He stared into his beer, clearly torn over whether to tell me. Finally, he took one last big gulp, and slammed the pint glass down on the table and started laughing.

"What's so funny?"

"Is silly," he slurred. "Is embarrassing."

"Embarrassing or not, it could keep you from being arrested."

He nodded, then shook his head, then nodded again. "I tell you, okay? I trapped in upstairs bathroom."

I leaned forward to be sure I'd heard correctly. "You were stuck in my bathroom?"

He nodded. "I need privacy, okay? I go up there for bathroom after you and Blisser come by. Urgent, okay?"

"Got it," I said, sitting back, not wanting too much detail now that I knew where he'd gone.

"But the lock jam," he continued. "Your house old and dumb, okay? The lock jam on me."

"That must have been very frustrating."

"Your house beautiful. Beautiful house. But dumb."

"Got it, my house is dumb, and you got locked in the bathroom. How long were you in there?"

"I don't know." He waved a dismissive hand. "Felt like long time. I break out after lights go out. I bust through door—sorry to hurt beautiful house—then I leave."

"So, you were stuck in the bathroom while Blister was rounding up people and telling them to leave for the day?"

"Suppose so." He eyed his empty glass. "When I come down, it dark and no one there so I leave. You want that?" He pointed to my beer.

I pushed it toward him to keep him talking. "Go ahead," I said. "Did you hear anything while you were upstairs?"

He tilted his head back and stared at the bar's ceiling. "Um... not sure. Maybe foosseps when I still using bathroom."

"Footsteps? What kind?" I leaned forward. "Heavy, light?"

Dimitri spread out his hands and looked at me with half-lidded eyes. "Don't know, okay? Foosseps. One, two, five—don't know. I too embarrassed to call out."

Before I could push, he threw his hands up in the air. "Oy, these Dodgers—they so lucky." Hank and Gus had also growled from the bar. Something must have happened on the television behind me.

I sighed. "All right, I'll leave you to finish the game. Thanks for the talk." I got up from the booth and headed for the door, waving goodbye to the guys at the bar.

"Hey lady," Dimitri called out to me before I got to the door. "You find those twins? They owe me hundred dollars."

No surprise there. "They owe everybody money," I said, and walked out.

Eighteen

NO OPPORTUNITY AROSE the rest of the day for me to ask the crew any more questions. They were each engrossed in their own tasks and Blister was flittering around like a gigantic bee checking on their progress.

I filled him in on Dimitri's suspended license when I got back to the house.

"I hate searching for subcontractors," said Blister, "and Dimitri will be hard to replace. He did good work—always sober, mind you. And I'll have to fill in until I get someone else."

"I trust you, Blister. Don't worry, you'll find someone."

Soon the day was ending, and the crew packed up to leave. Harper arrived just as the last of them headed out the door.

"Are you ready for tonight?" I asked her as we sat on the porch in the early evening.

"As ready as I'll ever be. Have you seen Mayor Dewey? Wouldn't be good if he didn't show up for his own debate."

"He's around here somewhere, I'm sure." Mayor Dewey was a frequent sight during the day, usually rustling around in the bushes, or napping on the porch, but he was nowhere to be found now.

Angie came around a little later, having had an early dinner with Roy.

"Have you seen Dewey?" Harper asked her.

"No, I thought he'd be with you."

"He'll turn up," I said. "He always does."

"I even brought him a little tie." Harper dug into her back pocked and pulled out a small blue collar with an attached tie. It read "Vote for MEow" down its length.

"How did the hunt go today?" asked Angie. "Did the crew come back?"

"Yes, and no incidents to report. Except Dimitri is off the crew because he lost his license. And it turns out he was stuck in my bathroom during the murder. He even broke the bathroom door trying to get out."

"Hmm," said Harper. "I really thought it could have been him—the nail gun and all."

I shook my head. "I doubt it. His story lined up. He did mention that the twins owed him money though, which is starting to sound repetitive."

"You think that could be a motive?" asked Angie.

"Why not? It's as good a motive as any right now."

"What about our encounter in the woods last night?" asked Harper. "Any thoughts on that?"

"Not yet. Hey, there he is." I pointed to the bush nearest the porch steps as Mayor Dewey stepped out and stretched before slowly walking over to Harper and rubbing her leg.

"Big night tonight, little guy," she said. "I brought you a gift." She put the collared tie on Dewey, and we all admired how distinguished he looked as he licked his paw.

"C'mon," Angie said. "It's almost time and we want to get there early."

Harper slung him under her arm and carried the furry, rotund candidate to the community center for the debate.

"Oh, lots of people," I said as we approached. "Are you ready Harper?"

"Me?" Harper stopping short.

"Yeah, aren't you going to be at the podium?" I asked.

"No way," she said cringing, shocked we'd even suggest such a thing. "I'm not here to debate."

"But Dewey can't talk," said Angie. "How's he going to answer the debate questions?"

"Don't worry about that. His job is to look cute and win hearts."

Angie and I exchanged glances, confused. "But I thought you'd been preparing for the debate this whole time?"

"I have." Harper patted the messenger bag at her hip. "Just in a... special way."

We entered through the double doors in the back of the room, like everyone else, but instead of taking a seat in the gallery, Harper, Angie and I sat at a table to the left of the two candidates' podiums. Mayor Jim and his team of none had reign over a table on the opposite side.

Harper set Dewey on the table and whispered into his ear, "Go around and rub on their legs." She nudged him off the table in the crowd's direction and he did as she ordered, seeking affection from the folks who'd already taken their seats.

"Look." I grabbed Harper's and Angie's attention and pointing to a small blonde woman in the front row. "There's Veronica Valentine. She's really running with this story."

"Excellent," said Harper. "Free press. I can't wait for the article to come out tomorrow."

Ryan arrived and I waved, but the place was already packed, so he found a seat on the far side of the room.

Deputy Todd, still in uniform, came up to the table and tapped on Harper's shoulder. "Would you wrangle that cat, please? We're going to start soon."

Harper nodded and searched the room for Mayor Dewey, who she finally spotted on Lovie's lap near the back row.

"Angie, would you grab a cup of water for him? I'm going to take him up to the podium."

"Sure." Angie disappeared to the snack and drink spread in the back. She grabbed a plastic cup of water and returned to the table.

Harper, meanwhile, had plucked Dewey from his adoring fans and carried him to his podium. It wasn't too steep for him to sit on, but as soon as she set him down, he batted around a pencil, eventually swatting it off the podium altogether. It was cute, but Harper frowned and motioned to Angie to abandon the water cup. Instead, she pulled out a few cat treats and left them on the podium for Dewey to snack on.

We watched as Harper pulled from her messenger bag a large sheet of butcher paper with all twenty-six letters of the alphabet written in large block letters. She taped the paper to the wall behind the podium then scooted Dewey and the podium back against the wall.

Mayor Jim watched all of this with pursed lips, a storm brewing behind his hooded eyes. No doubt he felt this was an affront to his years of public service.

Once Harper finished her set up, she returned to our table, but didn't sit down. She watched Dewey, probably hoping he wouldn't suddenly lose interest in all of this and leave.

Deputy Todd walked to the front of the room between the podiums and announced himself. "Good evening, everyone. I'm Deputy Todd Newman and I will act as impartial moderator for this, uh, debate." He glanced behind him to make sure both candidates were still there. Mayor Jim's nostrils flared, and Mayor Dewey nibbled on his treats.

"Tonight, we have incumbent mayor, Jim Thornen," Deputy Todd motioned behind him to Mayor Jim's side, "and challenger, Mayor—uh, Dewey the cat."

Harper clapped and whistled through her fingers, nearly deafening me. A few encouraging claps followed from the audience.

"Each candidate will have two minutes to introduce themselves and give a brief opening statement. Mayor Jim, we'll start with you." Deputy Todd stepped off to the side of the crowd to allow Jim an unobstructed view of the audience.

Mayor Jim's scowl suddenly turned to a sweet sugary smile. "Good evening, ladies and gentlemen. I'm so glad to see all your smiling faces out on this lovely night we're having. I'm sure you all know, but I'm your mayor, Jim Thornen, and I'm here tonight to talk about the issues that matter the most to you, our town's most beloved residents. As I have in the previous two terms, I will bring honor and vitality to our bustling little municipality. What this town needs is an experienced leader—someone who knows this town upside down and inside out and will fight for it. Do not throw your vote away. Do not make a mockery of your beloved town. I ask you tonight, to please honor me with your vote for mayor of Starry Cove."

"Thank you, Mayor." Deputy Todd said. "Now, uh, Dewey." He looked toward Harper, who shrugged him off. "Your turn, I guess."

Harper stepped off to the side to get a clearer look at the podium then pulled something out of her pocket and aimed it at the butcher paper. A red dot appeared on the sheet behind Dewey, who quickly spotted it and began following the dot with his eyes. Harper wiggled the dot over the letter H, waiting for Dewey to strike. Once he did, she moved the pointer to E, and Dewey struck again. Eventually, Dewey had spelled out H-E-L-L-O. Harper turned the laser pointer off and made a clicking noise with her mouth. Dewey turned back toward Harper and the crowd and began washing his paw.

The audience erupted in fits of giggles and some even clapped at the performance. A few of the ladies whispered among themselves in the back. I shook my head. Harper had figured out a way to let Dewey speak without speaking.

"Ridiculous," said Angie quietly beside me. "Incredible too."

"She's too clever for her own good," I whispered back. "If she's not careful, she'll find herself running this town."

Nineteen

I WOKE UP early the next morning, braved the drizzling rain to grab the newspaper off my front lawn and enjoyed a cup of coffee on my porch before the renovation horde arrived for the day. Last night was the first night I'd felt calm enough to sleep in my room upstairs—that and the idea of inflating and deflating my air mattress each day spurred me to just get over it already. The good news was I survived. No ghosts jumped out of the closet. No mysterious footsteps haunted my sleep. I was a big girl, and I could deal with this.

Dewey joined me on the porch and flopped down to nap at my feet. After his big night last night, he seemed even more eager to sleep through the day. I wondered what his days would be like as mayor. Would he simply stroll through town, receiving the adoration of his constituents, occasionally stopping to nap in someone's flower garden? Seemed like a pretty cushy job.

I flipped opened the newspaper, eager to read Veronica Valentine's latest article covering the debate last night. Sure enough, there it was at the bottom of the front page.

Darling Dewey's Delightful Debate

Starry Cove's resident cat, Dewey, melted hearts at last night's mayoral debate held at the town's local community center. Onlookers packed the venue like a can of sardines as they crowded in to get a peek at the Cove's curious candidate cat.

But what's a kitty to do when it comes to debating a human opponent? Leave that up to town mail carrier, Harper Tillman. Tillman has been spearheading Dewey's campaign from the start, and the debate was no exception. Preparation was key, she said, to ensuring Dewey's fans weren't left with crickets during questioning by the moderator, Sheriff's Deputy Todd Newman.

The solution, it seems, was simple. Tillman set Dewey in front of a poster of the alphabet and used a laser toy to lead him through spelling his answers, like a feline Ouija board.

Tillman shared her thoughts with me after the debate. "Dewey and I spent a lot of time preparing for the debate by testing out which lasers worked best for him. I'm really pleased with how it worked out."

Indeed, Tillman should be pleased. Polls taken at last night's debate showed Dewey up fifteen points on incumbent Mayor Jim Thornen, who eventually stormed out of the debate at the midway point after Dewey spelled out "more naps" as his answer to a question on his plan for improving residents' overall health and wellness. Tillman and Dewey capitalized on the opportunity of debating unchallenged to highlight a concerted effort on Dewey's part to reduce the town's rat population to zero. Free snuggles were also on the table to encourage residents to vote on election day, which rolls around on Thursday of this week.

I wondered if Mayor Jim could take much more of this. He nearly lost his head the previous night, storming out the double doors into the night, leaving the audience stunned. It certainly wasn't very becoming and could cost him votes in the end.

I leaned over and gave Mayor Dewey a scratch behind his ears. "No one likes a poor sport, do they?" He rubbed his chin on my hand, urging me to continue.

"You've found something, haven't you?"

My head shot up, and I searched the yard from where the voice had come. Greta stood along the walkway in the rain. Her long gray hair hung wet and limp over her shoulders and she stared straight at me, giving her a sinister vibe. I hadn't even noticed her walk up.

"What are you doing here?" I demanded.

"You've found something. I know you have. You and your friends have been searching."

"I want you to stay away from us." I stood up and backed away toward the front door. Dewey scrambled off as I moved, escaping to the bushes off the side of the porch. "I don't know what you're up to, but I want it to stop. No one needs to get hurt."

"I'm not here to hurt you, girl." Greta took a step forward.

"Stop," I said, holding up my hands. "Don't come any closer." Rain drenched Greta's dress, but it still hung loosely on her body—she could easily have a gun or other weapon hidden within the folds.

"I want to help you," she said. "Why won't you show me the notebook?"

"I want you to leave," I shouted. She'd taken another step toward the porch and I wasn't willing to let her get any closer. "Get off my property before I call the deputy."

Greta's face turned to stone then she scowled at me. "Suit yourself, foolish girl," she spat. "You think you know what you're doing, but you don't, and once you realize this, I'll be waiting." She turned away and returned down the walk toward the street, finally disappearing out of sight. I watched her go, unwilling to take my eyes off her until she was truly gone.

***

I'd retreated inside after Greta left, out of the rain and into the warm dry house. Blister finally arrived, and I breathed a sigh of relief at having him there with me should Greta decide she wanted to force the matter. The others arrived shortly after, except Cho, who wouldn't be working on electrical on a rainy day like today. I mostly tried to stay out of everyone's hair, but with nowhere to go in the rain, and my house taken up with renovations, I kept company with Blister in the early hours of the day.

"What are you working on?" I asked as Blister rustled through a stack of messy papers.

"The paperwork for Quentin." Blister held up a fistful of loose sheets. "I can't believe Edgar barely kept any notes or records on his apprenticeship."

"What does that mean?"

"It means I don't have much to go on. Quentin could only provide me with some records that he had copies of himself. I'll do my best though—he's counting on me."

"I'm sure you'll figure it out. You're doing a good thing helping Quentin out, and I'm sure he'll appreciate anything you can do for him."

"You're right," Blister said, looking around before lowering his voice. "It's just so frustrating. Like Edgar is badgering me from the grave, still causing trouble."

I left Blister to his paperwork and headed to the kitchen where I found Maisie resuming her work on the house's old plumbing.

"Good morning," I said, greeting her with a smile.

Maisie looked up from her tools, a lock of strawberry blonde hair hung over one eye and she blew it out of the way. "Morning."

"I'm glad you're back. I'm really excited to get moving on the changes to the house."

"I bet. It'll be a miracle if the whole thing doesn't

have to be replaced." She rifled through her toolbox before pulling out a wrench. "I can't wait to see what the bathrooms have in store for me."

I cringed. I wouldn't want to be in the room when she pulls out that old plumbing. Even though builders added the indoor plumbing after the house was originally constructed, it was antique and probably hadn't seen the light of day since it was first installed.

I leaned against the framing of the new counter which wobbled under my weight, so I quickly backed off and tried to look casual as I propped myself against the wall instead. "I hate to bring it up—"

"Then don't," she said, raising her eyes at me in warning.

Not to be deterred, I continued in another vein. "Well, I wanted to say some things are still bothering me about that day. Are you sure you saw nothing odd?"

"Will it make you leave me alone if I did?"

"I just want the truth, Maisie." I lowered my voice and looked around for others, then whispered, "There's still a killer on the loose."

She tilted her head to the side, considering my statement. After a moment of reflection, she said, "I guess it was weird that Cho was here that day."

"Cho?"

"That's right. It was raining buckets, like today. Not exactly the type of weather an electrician likes to work in, if you know what I mean."

I nodded as she continued to fiddle with a connector pipe.

She shook her head after a moment and put the pipe down. "I guess Blister could have asked her to come by for some reason, but Edgar and Quentin still had to frame out a wall before she could run wires, so I can't imagine what for. Maybe the basement." Maisie nodded toward the basement door in the kitchen.

"What about the basement?" Immediate concern coursed through me about anyone wandering around in the basement unprompted.

Maisie motioned toward where the sink used to be along the wall below the large original windows. "I was under the old sink counter working on your pipes—which were basically disintegrating in my hands, by the way. Anyway, I remember seeing Cho's legs and shoes—can't see much from that spot—as she came out from the basement door. She walked through the kitchen and out to the entryway. I just assumed she left."

"Do you know why she was down there?"

"I didn't even know she was here until then, let alone why she'd be down in the basement."

"When was this?" I asked, trying to piece it together in my head.

"A little while before Blister called it a day. The power going out doesn't bother me." She tapped the light strapped around her head. "But it's a real nuisance for everyone else."

I must have been staring off because Maisie asked, "Can I get back to work, then? These rusty pipes aren't going to replace themselves."

"Yeah, sorry. Thanks for the help. I hope your kids are doing okay."

"Thanks. Hey, Poppy," she called to me as I turned away. "You remember how I told you Dimitri thought Edgar stole money from him?"

"Yeah."

She dropped her eyes. "I think he really stole it. Edgar had already given me the exact amount Dimitri claimed he stole—Edgar said it was for back due child support. I guess he wanted to do right by the kids. I didn't say anything before because we really needed the money." Maisie hadn't lifted her eyes off the pipes in her lap as she confessed this to me.

"I understand. I won't say anything. Besides, something tells me Dimitri would want it to go to the kids anyway."

"Thanks. I hope you're right."

I was about to walk away when I remembered what she'd asked me before. "Did you ever get your money from Dustin and Justin?"

She nodded. "Yeah. They gave me the hundred bucks yesterday. If that was your doing, thanks."

"Probably not, but at least you got it. Thanks for the talk, Maisie."

"No problem," she said. "I hope you figure this all out. My kids deserve answers."

***

I found the twins in the living room, taking drywall measurements. "You guys finally made it out of the rain I see."

"Yeah," said Justin. "With no Dimitri, Blister asked us to measure some drywall so he could get it installed."

I propped myself up against a sawhorse. "Seems you two owe a lot of money."

They both looked offended, but I didn't miss the subtle glance they'd shared. "We just paid Maisie yesterday," said Dustin, "so we don't know what you mean."

I played the only card I had. "I can go to the authorities. If you've been fleecing people, they won't be too happy to hear it. The deputy and I are good friends, you know." A little white lie, perhaps. Deputy Todd and I were technically on speaking terms, which was close enough.

This prompted another, longer, shared glance between the twins. A moment later, Justin said, "Don't worry about it. Everyone will get their money. It's just a game, after all."

"You said you don't play fantasy but you ask a lot of questions. Are you sure you don't want to get in on the action? The buy in is just—"

"Let me guess," I said, cutting him off, "a hundred dollars?"

"That's right," said Justin, now eyeing me suspiciously. "A hundred dollars."

"How stupid do you two think I am?" I folded my arms, hoping I came across as commanding and strong-willed. "You need my hundred dollars to pay off the others. What kind of pyramid scheme do you have going here?"

Dustin turned to Justin and I could see the gears turning in their heads. Would they bolt? Try to overpower me? I wondered where Blister was and cursed myself for slipping away from him. But I had them trapped, in a way. They'd have to tell me everything now that I'd figured out their plan.

"Did Edgar figure it out?" I asked, cautiously. "Is that why you were fighting the day he was killed?"

"We didn't kill him," Justin said quickly. "Yes, okay, we were fighting about the fantasy league we were running, but we didn't kill anyone. Why would we even be upstairs?"

"Because that's where Edgar was." I backed up toward the entrance to the foyer, to a spot where I wouldn't be so alone with these two.

"Why would Edgar be upstairs?" asked Dustin. "We weren't due to work on that part of the house until we completed the kitchen."

"He—" I stumbled on my own thinking. Why had Edgar gone upstairs? Was he looking for someone—or something?

"That's right," said Justin. "And don't forget, we were covered in mud. We would have tracked it all over the house."

"Yeah," added Dustin. "Did you find a bunch of muddy boot prints?"

"No, I—"

"Of course you didn't. Because we weren't even allowed in the house that day, remember? We got to enjoy our time in the endless rain and muck."

They were both staring me down now. I'd come in guns blazing with accusations, only to be put back in my place by the twins. Their logic was solid. I had found no muddy prints that day and they were covered with it, head to toe. I'd even taken off my own wet shoes so as not to track anything in, so they certainly weren't traipsing around the house.

"All right," I said finally. "It wasn't you two. But you're still conning people with your fantasy league games. That must stop, or I *will* go to the authorities."

Another shared glance. They must have a secret language, only using their eyes to communicate with one another. "Okay," said Justin. "Fantasy isn't lucrative anyway, and we've got other means to make a living."

"Like finishing your work here," I said forcefully, and left the room quickly on my own terms before they could respond.

The twins had left me a lot to think about, not the least was Edgar's mysterious presence upstairs. There was no work being done in the upstairs bedrooms, and Dimitri had only gone up there to find a more private bathroom in which to relieve himself. Otherwise, there was no reason for anyone to be in the rooms above.

I had to consider the worst. Edgar had been upstairs, that much is fact. But the reason he was up there left me cold. Had Greta been right? If there were a spy in the mix like she claimed, had *Edgar* been that spy?

***

"Edgar?" Harper wondered. "That'd be pretty wild."

Angie shrugged. "I guess it's possible."

The three of us gathered on my front porch in the late afternoon and I'd filled them in on the day's events. The rain had continued, but the forecast was looking up for tomorrow—possible sun.

"And you said Greta just appeared in the rain, like a specter?"

I nodded and pointed out toward the walkway and trellis. "She was halfway up the walk before I realized she was there. Dewey took off like a rocket."

"But it obviously wasn't Edgar shooting at us in the forest, so who was it?"

"Maybe the same person who killed him?" Angie offered.

"I don't know why though. It's all still a muddle. I got some more information today about who *didn't* kill Edgar."

"Oh yeah?"

"I'm pretty sure the twins weren't involved. They were so muddy and gross that day, there's no way they could have gone upstairs without leaving a total mess in their wake."

Harper tapped her lip. "Makes sense."

Angie nodded. "They would have dripped everywhere."

"And Maisie shared some interesting information." They leaned in closer, waiting for me to continue. "She said that Cho was sniffing around in the basement that day."

"The basement?" asked Angie, shocked. "What would she want in the basement? That's where…"

"Right," I said. "It's highly suspicious, especially since Maisie said Cho shouldn't have been working that day, on account of the rain."

"That's a bit of a leap. There're loads of reasons she could have been down there. And none that have to do with… you know."

I leveled a stern look at Harper and she cut off, a reminder of our previous discussion regarding Cho. She cast her eyes downward at my subtle rebuke. "It's possible that it's nothing," I said finally. "But if it's not raining tomorrow, she should be on site. Then I can get answers from the horse's mouth."

Dewey wandered around the corner of the porch, a

bit wet but he had otherwise survived the day's storm.

"Come here, little guy." Harper lifted him up into her arms. She dried him off with her sweatshirt. "Big day for you tomorrow."

"You two put on a real performance last night," I said. "The *Vista View* article this morning was practically glowing."

"I've got another after-party planned at Shelby's Diner tomorrow night, too. After he wins."

"What if he doesn't win?" asked Angie.

Harper looked offended. "He's going to win. And if he doesn't, well, we'll go to Jim's party and partake of the free food and drinks."

"That sounds about right." I smiled. Harper would always find a way to stick it to Mayor Jim somehow.

"But he won't lose. The polls have him up by fifteen points."

Angie tutted. "Those polls aren't scientific."

"Whatever," said Harper dismissively as she nuzzled Mayor Dewey, who purred softly in her arms. "After tomorrow night, this town's going to have a new mayor calling the shots, and he's the cutest, fuzziest little dude in the whole county."

Twenty

DAWN BROKE TO clear skies on election day. The salty air wafted up the cliff from the ocean below, but the sun broke through the clouds and fog early, leaving a morning kissed with warmth.

I enjoyed my coffee on the porch, as usual, and waited for the crew to arrive. Blister arrived first—also as usual—followed by Maisie, Cho, Quentin, and the twins, ready to start the workday. I greeted each as they arrived and shared the news of the upcoming election party tonight and invited them all to attend. The mention of free food, drinks, and especially pie seemed to perk each of them up, so I was almost certain that they'd show up to the party. Blister promised to be there outright to support our friend, but probably more so to spend time with Angie, who I mentioned would be there all night along with Harper and me.

I followed them inside after I finished my coffee and found Cho in the foyer working on one of the electrical boxes in the wall. She leaned over the only small table I'd left for use, teetering on one booted toe. Her denim overalls were scuffed on the knee, having seen better days, but her long-sleeve shirt was unwrinkled and ready to take on the day's abuses.

"Glad to have you back. We missed you yesterday."

"Unlike the twins who roll around in the mud like pigs, I don't work in the rain." She turned her screwdriver into the screws of the outlet. "Way too dangerous."

"But you're back today. Things are still a bit wet."

Cho glanced at me wryly and said, "I'd never get anything done in this climate if I didn't take advantage of the breaks in the weather."

"I'm happy you're back, though. I've had a chance to talk with the others, but not really with you."

"About what?"

"Mostly to find out what you remembered about the day Edgar died."

"I thought we talked about that," said Cho, grunting a little as she continued fiddling with the outlet.

"Maybe a little, sure. But others have mentioned how keen you were to be on this project and about how you wanted to know who was on the crew."

"Yeah, that's right." She straightened up, finished with—or at least taking a break from—the outlet screws. "It's not weird to want to know who you're working with."

"And the interest in the house?"

"This house?" she responded. "It's an old house, you know—one of the oldest in the county, and definitely the oldest in this town. Old houses have strange wiring, usually installed after the house was first built."

"I know the house is really, really old. I'm not sure

about the wiring though."

"Well, that's my job," she said, grabbing a different tool out of her toolbox on the floor. "Which means, I needed to do some research into wiring as ancient as yours. If it isn't installed at the time the house is built, there're often workarounds the installers did that can cause issues down the line, especially when making changes like you are now."

It made sense, and the house was definitely the oldest building in the town, even older than the stone church, which was built to look old rather than having true age itself. I'm sure the wiring was unique and daunting to anyone tasked with working on them. But that didn't explain why she was in the basement. "Maisie said she saw you in the basement that day, and that you weren't supposed to be here."

Cho stopped working on the wall outlet and turned to me. "So what?"

I got the distinct feeling Cho didn't like my questions any longer, but this was the time to press it and find out what she was hiding, if anything. "You said you don't like working in rain. So why were you here?"

She spread her arms out wide. "Look, this is a big house, lots of wiring, and you want a lot of power running through these walls once we're done. I don't have the luxury of just taking days off every time it rains, so I came over that day to get a closer look at the electrical layout."

"What does that have to do with the basement?" I asked.

Cho huffed and looked at me askance, as though the answer were obvious. "Haven't you noticed? Since the house was wired after it was built, most of the wires are still fully exposed in the basement—they aren't built into the structure down there. It's like a puzzle I have to figure out."

The basement was a mess of wires and junk. I guess my eyes just scanned over the cords that ran along the walls and ceiling beams down there as if they didn't exist. But it seems they actually *do* something, and Cho needed to find out.

"So that's why I was in the basement that day." She leaned down and swapped out her tool again. "I couldn't work on the electrical, but I could work on mapping the electrical layout and compare it to the most recent plans you have for the house."

"That makes sense now that you mention it," I said. "I guess I never thought about what makes this house tick."

Cho smiled. "That's why you hired us, right?"

I nodded, feeling better about the whole thing. It was a relief to have Blister and his crew back and working on modernizing the mansion. I'd been so eager to get it started and finished that I was swimming in doubt and spotting suspects in every nook and cranny. The twins had shut me down yesterday, and now Cho was also losing patience with me. But that didn't mean there wasn't still a killer among us, and that grated on me. Even if Edgar was a royal jerk, he didn't deserve to die. And worse, two kids lost their dad that day. I couldn't simply let it go. I had to find the means to get whoever was responsible to out themselves, one way or another.

***

I still brooded on my failure to discover the killer when

Harper, Angie, and I arrived at the community center where the night's election was to be held. Harper cradled Dewey under her zipped-up sweater to protect him from the rain that started falling as the sun set.

"How does this work?" I asked, as we stepped into the shelter of the room. We threw off our coats and hung them up to dry on the back wall.

"What do you mean?" asked Harper.

"I didn't receive a ballot or anything. How do I vote?"

"Oh, that. You'll see."

Angie winked at me. "We do things special here in Starry Cove. Traditions, that sort of thing."

Shelby walked by and Harper caught her by the arm. "Is everything squared away for afterward?"

"Yes, dearie," said Shelby, giving Dewey a little scratch behind the ears. "Everything is ready to go. Good luck tonight."

"Thanks. Don't forget to vote for Dewey," Harper squeaked out the side of her mouth, waving Dewey's little paw as Shelby left to find a seat.

"Wow," said Angie, looking around at the crowd. "It feels like everyone is here. I thought the late start to the rain might keep some of them away. Roy's here somewhere, too. No doubt boasting to the guys about the new staff we're bringing on."

"Do we get in line? Everyone's milling around."

"Nope." Angie shook her head. "You'll see. But we should find our seats soon." We scanned the room and Angie led us to three open seats in a row of chairs near the back.

"How did today go?" Harper asked me once we sat

down. Dewey, wearing his special tie, curled up lazily on her lap and promptly closed his eyes for a nap.

"I had time to talk to Cho."

"And?"

"She was checking out the house's wiring layout in the basement."

"Hmm," said Angie. "I guess that makes sense."

"See, I told you. There're a ton of wires down in that basement. I can't imagine anyone except Cho could figure them out."

"Well, it answers our question about the basement at least."

"There's Veronica." Harper pointed to the front row. "Here to continue reporting on her exclusive scoop, no doubt."

"She has a camera guy with her this time," I said. "You and Dewey may get your pictures in the paper."

Harper's face dropped. "I didn't think about that. I don't want my picture anywhere."

"Don't worry. You have to give permission, I think. Anyway, she'll probably only want a picture of Dewey. And he looks so cute in the little tie you made him."

"What is *that*?" I asked. A large leather-bound trunk had come into my view on the folding table at the front of the room. It's opening faced away from me, so I couldn't get a good look, but even from this distance and viewpoint I could tell it was extremely old, the leather cracking. Thick straps wrapped around its girth, secured tightly at the top by enormous metal buckles, their sheen faded with age.

"Oh good," said Angie. "They brought it out already."

"Brought what out? It looks like an old treasure chest."

"It's always looked like that."

Angie continued, "It's the box we use to cast our ballots. Everyone gets in line to vote and drops their ballots in the Starry Cove election box—that's what it is, by the way. They stand over the box and say, 'By right, my share,' and drop it into the slot that's carved in the top. Then it goes to the next person, and so on until everyone's voted."

"*By right, my share*," I repeated. "What does that mean?"

"I don't really know," said Angie. "We've just always said it. It's our tradition, and this town loves its traditions."

"You have to say it, too," Harper warned. "One year, I forgot and just plunked my ballot into the box. Well, you'd have thought I'd shot Mayor Dewey with the way the election committee threw up their hands and blustered like a flock of decapitated chickens."

"But you don't know what it means? It's such an odd saying."

"Nope. Maybe it's something about your share of the vote being counted or something like that."

"Yeah," said Angie. "It's probably something like that."

"Sounds kind of pirate-y, though, don't you guys think? And that trunk…"

"Oh." Angie stared at the box curiously. "Now that you mention it—and after everything we've seen—it does sound like something pirates would say."

"I just know the drama of *not* saying it is not worth

the headache. And there are no gold doubloons in that trunk. Trust me, I've peeked. It's just votes."

The clock on the wall ticked over to seven o'clock and a few people got up and formed a line along the outer edge of the room. Deputy Todd grabbed a microphone from the podium and announced to the room that voting would begin.

"Let's let the line die down a bit before we go up," said Angie.

"Dewey doesn't get to vote—can you believe that?" Harper stared at Mayor Jim as he got in line behind Bea Trotter. "Mayor Jim gets to vote, but not Dewey. It's a disgrace."

"It'll be fine. Remember the polls?"

Harper nodded. "I know. I think my nerves are getting to me."

"Do we find out the results tonight?" I asked. "How do the votes get counted?"

Angie giggled at my curiosity. "Don't worry. The election team counts the ballots right here. We have to wait until at least nine though, so they can be sure everyone who wants to vote gets the opportunity."

"That's what the refreshments table is for." Harper nodded toward a table along the back where a few people were already partaking of the snacks. "If there's one thing about Starry Cove, it's that food must be served at all gatherings."

"Once they count the ballots," Angie continued, "they'll count them again to be sure. Then Deputy Todd will announce the winner. The last few times, it's just been Mayor Jim running, so this is pretty exciting."

Lovie Newman was the first person in line, and I

watched as she finished filling out her ballot and stepped up to the trunk.

"By right, my share," Lovie announced clearly, then dropped her ballot through the slot in the top and made way for the next person. Shelby stepped up next, gave Dewey a sly wink, and repeated the words. The line continued in this manner as each person said the words then dropped their ballot into the chest.

Ryan appeared next to us after a few voters had cast their ballots, looking confused. "What is happening?"

"I forgot you're new too," said Angie. "It's a bit of a tradition."

"Don't worry," I told him. "I'll walk you through it. Should we all head up?"

Harper nodded, Dewey still napping on her lap. "I'll carry him. Poor guy is all tuckered out. It's been a long week."

The line shuffled slowly, but eventually it was my turn to cast my vote. A member of the election team handed me a ballot and give me a small private space to fill it out. While Mayor Jim was not exactly my cup of tea, I still found it odd to consider voting for a cat. My pen hovered over Dewey's name, then back to Mayor Jim, before finally bubbling in next to Dewey. In the end, I wasn't voting for a cat. I was voting for someone I knew had it in her to make a difference—Harper. Before stepping up to the trunk, I glanced at the line behind me and gave Harper a confident smile. She waved Dewey's paw back at me.

The trunk seemed even larger up close, and even more rustic than I'd initially thought. Its wooden sides transformed into a dark, warm patina and the leather straps had cracked and crumbled in places. Massive hinges rusted into what looked like oak, giving the piece a sense of age that no one could fake or replicate.

"By right, my share," I said, dropping my ballot into the top slot. No magical feeling came over me—no sense of transformation. Angie joined me quickly after casting her own ballot, and finally Harper and Ryan.

"Now, we wait," Angie said to Ryan and me.

"Snack time," said Harper, who carried Dewey perched in one arm so she could have the other free to browse the refreshments.

"She seems in excellent spirits," said Ryan.

"She should. I'm pretty sure she's going to win tonight."

"Dewey as our mayor. What a strange thought," said Angie. "Still, probably an improvement."

I glanced at Mayor Jim, who sat silently in a chair against the wall. He had a small cup of water in his hand and stared forward, as though he knew his days were numbered.

"It looks as though he's resigned to his fate," I said, indicating the mayor. "He fought against the wrong candidate."

"He didn't fight much at all," said Ryan.

Angie shook her head sadly. "Why would he? I can't blame him for thinking it was silly to compete—even debate—against a cat."

"That's where he went wrong, though. He wasn't competing against a cat for votes—he was competing against Harper."

"What do you mean? Dewey's running, not Harper. Remember? She didn't want to."

"She said she didn't want to, but I bet every person who cast a vote for Dewey tonight was really casting a vote for her. Dewey's just a proxy."

Angie turned to the refreshment table, where Harper was grazing. We watched as people would tap her arm and whisper supportive words, smile, shake her free hand, wish her well.

"Maybe someone should tell her?" Angie wondered.

"Nah," I said. "She's in a good place with Dewey as her buffer. Besides, she hasn't won yet."

We waited patiently for the voting to end. The election panel sat in one corner counting the ballots in silence, occasionally whispering among themselves. Then they recounted each one. Harper had eventually let Dewey down and he now mingled with the crowd while she lingered in the back of the room. The closer the clock ticked to nine, the more her previous good spirits transformed into frantic paces. I waved her over and motioned for her to take a seat next to me.

"I can't seem to stop worrying," she said, sliding into the chair. "What if he doesn't win?"

"Then he doesn't win." I put a reassuring arm around her. "And the world moves on."

"Oh no, here comes Deputy Todd. Where's Dewey?" Harper's head whipped around the room, searching for a fluffy ball of ginger cat.

"I saw him by the back doors a minute ago," said Angie, "trying to get Pastor Basil to share his cookies."

Deputy Todd's voice boomed over the microphone, "Would the candidates please come up?"

Harper looked around frantically. Finally, Lovie and Shelby called her over. Dewey, apparently, had found a spot to nap in the corner on top of someone's jacket. He meowed in protest as she picked him up and carried him to the front of the room.

Mayor Jim stared in disgust as Harper and Dewey took their spot next to him. Harper returned his glare. "Let the best cat win."

"You'll regret this," he snarled under his breath.

Deputy Todd hushed them both, then returned to the microphone. "I will now read the results." He walked to the election committee and they handed him an envelope. Everyone waited in silence as he slowly returned to the center of the room in front of the two candidates. He fumbled awhile opening the envelope, adding to the suspense. A trickle of sweat ran down the side of Mayor Jim's face. Harper nuzzled her face in Dewey's fur.

Deputy Todd cleared his throat. "The mayor of Starry Cove is... Dewey the cat."

Harper's eyes popped open and Jim's squeezed shut as he slinked off into the shadows in defeat. Veronica, standing nearby the candidates, whispered energetically into her recorder and waved the cameraman closer for a better shot.

Shouts of "Mayor Dewey" and "Hurray for Dewey" erupted from the crowd. I had expected this outcome, but the volume in the enclosed community center still made me to cover my ears. At the sudden commotion, even Dewey, normally so relaxed, bolted from Harper's arms and out the back doors into the rain, leaving her standing alone in the front of the room. She looked around at the crowd, cheering her on. Tears streamed down her face as Angie and I rushed to her side.

"You did it," Angie said. "You beat Mayor Jim."

"*Former* Mayor Jim." She was all grins. "I can't believe it."

"You were great," I said, beaming. I was truly proud of my friend, who'd accomplished this through hard work and determination.

Shelby appeared at her side. "Congratulations, Harper. I'll head to the diner to get ready for the party."

"Thanks Shelby."

"Way to go, Harper," said another resident before another shouted, "Nice work, see you at the party."

It felt like every resident came by to congratulate Harper and wish her well. She thanked each of them in turn, shaking their hands, saying how excited she was for the future and reminded them about the party, while Mayor Dewey, for his part, was nowhere in sight.

Twenty-one

THE ENTIRE TOWN, save for Jim Thornen, trooped through the rain across the street to Shelby's Diner, where a celebratory spread covered the breakfast counter for all to enjoy. We burst through the diner door, dragging in sopping wet jackets and shoes, but Shelby, who'd already arrived, didn't seem to mind.

The atmosphere was jovial, and the residents used this opportunity to chat and make predictions on Mayor Dewey's first initiatives. Angie and I hung back after arriving, quickly grabbing a drink and some hors d'oeuvres before retreating to the quiet serenity of a booth at the back of the restaurant.

"Why so glum?" Angie asked me as we watched the partygoers.

"Glum?"

"Yeah, your face is all droopy, like you're sad or something."

My face must have betrayed my thoughts. "I'm still wondering about the house—about Greta and the killer.

It's exciting that Dewey's won, but there's still so much unresolved."

"Do you have any ideas on who it could be? You've picked at it so much you must have some clue."

"As soon as I think I do, I'm right back where I started. I think the only way to find out who killed Edgar is to make them betray themselves."

"How can we do that?"

"I'm working on it. I need a little more time, and hopefully some inspiration."

Angie suddenly perked up. "There's Blister," she said cheerily. "Blister, over here." He spotted her quickly and headed our way after swiping a cookie off the table.

"Nice party," he said, standing over our booth. "Thanks for the invite, even though I don't live here."

"Don't be silly," said Angie. "You're family."

"The others should be here too. Everyone was keen on making it tonight. Free pie will bring out the dead, even in this rain." As if on cue, thunder cracked outside and a bright flash of lightning soon after illuminated the diner. "Summer always brings the strangest weather."

Harper emerged from the crowd holding Mayor Dewey and walked over to our booth. "I found this guy trying to stay dry under a bush outside. That's no place for our new mayor, is it?" She hugged him tightly to her chest then set him down on the tile floor. "Now, go schmooze the constituency." She patted his fuzzy orange behind to get him moving and he scampered back into the crowd.

"How are things going?" asked Angie.

"Great," Harper said, staring after the cat. "The entire town is here, and everyone is really excited to have Mayor

Dewey—no fear of using that title now—in charge of the town's affairs. They're asking me all sorts of interesting questions."

"I bet." I shared a subtle smile with Angie.

"Congratulations on your win, Harper," said Blister. "I heard it was a doozy."

"Thanks. Dewey was great about the whole thing."

Mayor Dewey, we saw, had climbed up on the snack table and sniffed a platter of crab cakes. Behind him the crowd fawned and pointed at how adorable he was, laughing among themselves and having a good time. The diner door opened, and the sound of the rain poured in, reminding us how bad the storm had gotten. It was Cho, who looked around on her tip toes over the sea of heads until she spied the table of free food.

"Oh good," said Blister. "Cho made it through the storm."

"I might pop over and say hello." This time, Harper didn't look my way before heading off, avoiding any potential admonishment. On her way back to the crowd, she stepped around Shelby, who was winding her way around the tables toward our side party.

"Great party, Shelby," Angie said. "Everything is perfect. Thanks again for helping out Harper."

"It's no trouble, dearie. Besides, it's good old-fashioned business. Harper's given me a mind to dip my toe into catering."

"Oh?" Angie inquired. "What type of catering exactly?"

"Don't worry, Angie. I won't cut into your bakery. But that doesn't mean we can't come up with a mutually beneficial partnership." Shelby gave Angie a wink, eliciting a nod of approval.

"There's Quentin and the twins," said Blister. "I need to talk to him about re-doing some framing. I'll talk to you ladies later." Blister wandered off toward the new arrivals.

"Blister," I shouted after him. He stopped and turned to me. "Don't let those two ply their fantasy games here. I have a feeling they thought this might be a place to shoot fish in a barrel." Blister nodded and turned away.

"Shop talk at a party?" Shelby shook her head. "It ought to be a crime."

"You're one to talk, Shelby."

"It's not really shop talk. Blister's taken on Quentin as his apprentice. After Edgar... you know."

"Oh, right," said Angie. "That was nice of him."

"Maybe we should join the party, too?"

"C'mon, get up," said Shelby urging us out of the booth. "We don't bite. Have some fun."

"I'm not really a party person." Angie eyed the sizable crowd. "It makes me nervous."

"You've been in front of crowds before, remember? And you survived."

"Okay..." Angie said as I dragged her into the throngs of people to socialize and support Harper's achievement.

Maisie chimed through the door a while later, sharing with me that she had to find a babysitter, but wanted to see this cat she's been reading about in the newspaper.

I pointed her toward the snack table. "He's over there. Help yourself."

"Thanks," was all she said before beelining to the snacks.

I joined Blister, who had accumulated a pack of the renovation crew around him.

He was in the middle of telling a story. "And then, the guard shook his head and led me out. Oh, hi Poppy. I was telling these guys about my time in the slammer."

"The county jail is hardly the slammer," said Angie, who'd overheard the ending and appeared beside me.

"Well, it—" he blustered. "It was a life-changing experience."

Harper joined us too, sliding into the group beside Cho and exchanging a smile with her as the others made room. The crew was all together, minus Dimitri, whom I'd left well enough alone. As I looked around, I realized that one of these cheerful faces could still be the murderer of Edgar Biggs.

"I'm telling you," Blister continued, "you don't want to spend a single night in jail. It's cold, lonely... Heck, there wasn't even a T.V. for me to watch."

"I wonder if they've identified any more suspects?" asked Cho.

Blister shook his head. "Not that I'm aware of. Deputy Todd sure is dragging his heels on this one."

"Wait," I said aloud, an idea sparking in my brain. I grabbed Angie's hand and squeezed. "They did find a clue, I think."

"They did?" Angie asked, bewildered at the sudden mention of new information.

"That's right," I said, squeezing her hand again. "I told you earlier." Harper watched us cautiously, cluing in on the intensity of my voice.

"Oh, that's right. They found a clue," Angie said slowly, finally catching on. "What was it again?"

"They said they found something at the house. Something that would solve the murder and that they needed to take more samples tomorrow."

"Oh, that's right." Angie nodded, trying her best not to still look confused.

"What do you mean they found something?" asked Cho. "What did they find?"

"I'm not sure," I said, shrugging. "Only that they'd be by the house tomorrow to collect it. Told me to stay out of the upstairs bedroom."

"Then we'll finally know what happened to Edgar," said Blister. "That'll be good news."

"Yeah, great," said Maisie. "We can all finally move on."

"I hope they don't come too early. The three of us"—I indicated Harper and Angie—"will be here all night helping Shelby clean up after the party."

"Yeah," said Harper. "We'll be here *really* late."

"Gosh," said Angie. "Roy will have to open the bakery tomorrow by himself. I'm sure I'll be too tired."

Blister looked around at the pilfered table of snacks, the streamers hanging from the ceiling, the spills on the floor. "Sounds like a good time," he chuckled. "Too bad we'll all be long gone."

The crew laughed. Harper, Angie, and I laughed too, although more mechanically. We'd laid the bait—a definitive clue, a vacant house—now we waited to see who would bite.

The party wound down about midnight—an ordinance someone had already brought to Harper and Mayor Dewey's attention. We hung back along with Shelby, who'd already carried dishes back into the kitchen. "The boys will take care of these tomorrow," she shouted back to us, dumping a load of plates into the commercial-sized kitchen sink. "It'll be bikini weather at the North Pole before I take up doing dishes again."

The last of the guests made their way out the door, braving the rain, thunder, and lightning. Cho was one of the last to leave and waved back at Harper as she grabbed her rain jacket and left. Harper returned the wave with a beaming smile.

"Well," said Angie, elbowing Harper and grinning up at her. "That seemed to go well."

Harper stared after Cho, her face no longer smiling.

"What is it?" Angie asked, her cheerfulness now turned to concern.

"I thought I saw something." Harper shook her head, unsure.

Shelby rumbled through the swivel kitchen doors. "Gather up the tablecloths, will you, dearies?"

Harper moved slowly to collect the fabric coverings. Something was bothering her.

"What is it?" I finally asked.

Harper shook her head again, her brow furrowed, and whispered to Angie and me, "I remember where I saw the Gold Hand symbol."

"What?" Angie looked around the diner as if we'd be overheard.

"I saw it again tonight," Harper continued, "on Cho's arm when she waved at me. Her *tattoos*. She's got one on her wrist of the same symbol we saw in the notebook." Harper pointed to a spot just above her right wrist. "I must have seen it before when we'd first met—when we were cleaning up Poppy's spilled coffee."

"Cho…" I worked it through my mind. Then I remembered. "Shelby," I shouted across the diner. Shelby looked up from cleaning a table on the other side of the room. "Remember when you told me a lady came in asking about Arthur and the house?"

"Sure, do, dearie. I hope you were able to help her out."

"Was she an older woman or younger?"

"Well, dearie, it was that nice young lady I saw you talking to earlier." Shelby pondered this a moment. "Cho, I think her name was. Yes, that sounds right."

"Cho asking about Arthur," said Angie. "That sounds bad."

"Really bad," said Harper. She looked ill.

"I need to get to the house," I said, throwing the stack of used plastic cups I'd been collecting onto the table. "Slatherby's book is still there—I've got to get it." I moved toward the door, but Angie caught my arm.

"What about Cho?" she asked with pleading eyes. "She could be dangerous. If she killed Edgar…"

"We can't wait, Angie. She could already be at the house." I ran out the diner door and into the rain. Shelby called out behind me, but I couldn't make out what she'd said.

"Poppy, wait!" Harper shouted after me, but my feet continued to move, splashing through puddles, the need to preserve Arthur's secrets urged me on. A flash of lightning lit up the road, and the crack of thunder right after spurred me on as I ran from the diner toward the mansion. Rain pelted my face, but I could still make out the house, looming at the end of the street. Each burst of lightning illuminated the structure, lending it a menacing and sinister aura. And I was running right for it.

Twenty-two

AS I REACHED the property from the road, my strides took me directly to the front door which remained closed and locked the way I'd left it earlier in the evening. I caught my breath before lurking around the porch to the back door off the kitchen. This, I found, showed evidence of being broken. Searching around the porch, I found a cache of Maisie's new PVC pipes—the replacements for the old rusted ones she hated so much—and gripped one of the shorter lengths tightly in my hand. My weapon wasn't much, and the thick hard plastic would do nothing but distract if I struck anyone with it, but it was better than no protection at all. I slowly opened the door, careful not to let the hinges squeak too loudly. The kitchen appeared empty except for the puddles dotting the floor where the intruder must have passed through.

Creeping past the wet patches, I checked the light switch on the other end of the room, pipe held high ready to attack anyone who may jump out at me. No lights flickered on. The power must be out again—or Cho was playing tricks.

I stepped silently into the foyer and through to the living room, where Arthur's old sofa remained as the sole piece of furniture in the room. My backpack sat beside the sofa and I quickly checked its contents for Slatherby's book. My heart sank—the book was gone. Slatherby's book and all its information, including my notes, was now in the hands of an enemy. Despite this loss, I tried to consider that it could have been worse—at least she didn't have the notebook. I closed my eyes and thanked my lucky stars it was still safely locked away in Vista.

A bump upstairs caught my attention. My eyes flashed open. She was still here, upstairs in one of the bedrooms, possibly searching for the mysterious clue I'd fabricated earlier in the evening.

I gripped the pipe tighter in my hand and crept up the stairs, following the trail of water. At the top of the staircase, another flash of lightning lit up the second-floor landing, revealing wet prints that led straight to my bedroom. Rustling came from inside the dark room as I flattened myself against the wall by the open door—items tossed out of my closet and drawers pulled out of their casing. Unless this person had night vision, it was too dark to look for anything, they must be trying to destroy whatever clue remained instead.

My heart beat hard and fast, I thought for sure it would leap right out of my chest and flop on the floor. Thunder crashed outside, and I jumped in my own skin. It was now or never. I took a deep breath and squeezed my eyes shut for a moment, steeling myself to what was to come.

With determination, I shifted my body away from the

wall and through the open doorway. Movement by the bed drew my eye. Before I could raise the pipe, a figure crashed into me, throwing me back. I stumbled into the door, closing it as I fell to the floor, trapping us both in the room. My eyes blurred from the impact as a flash of lightning blazed through the window. The hooded figure crouched, looked at me against the closed door, then back to the window. A new escape route had appeared. I eased myself up, shaken from the force of the fall, one leg, then the other. Glass shatter and I turned to the window in time to see the shadow disappear into the driving rain. I shook the haziness from my head and stumbled to the broken sill.

I slowly eased myself out of the window, ready for an attack that never came. Instead, I spied a dark shadow scaling the roof tiles up and to my left, headed to the top. One foot slipped and a jumble of tiles slid past me and straight off the roof, landing in the bushes far below.

Intending to follow, I needed a safer way. In this rain and with my weapon in one hand, I wouldn't be able to catch myself if I should slip. To the right of the broken window, a decorative rail followed the line of the roof up the slope. I unlocked the latch on the window and eased it open, allowing the frame and loose glass to fall away. One step onto the ledge, I tested the grip of my shoes. It seemed okay. Another step and I was out in the rain, holding onto the side of the house with one hand, pipe still gripped in the other. The rail was a good six feet from where I stood but would work well as a ladder up to the top. I flicked the rain out of my eyes and took a leap of faith across the gap. The fingers of my free hand grasped onto the railing tightly and I hugged myself to the rail, thankful I'd made it.

Now, I needed to follow the rail up the roofline to the top. More tiles dribbled off the edge on the other side of the window where the shadow had retreated. The dark figure was still struggling up the wet, slanted tiles. I wasn't too far behind.

As I reached the top, which flattened out to a narrow length spanning the entire house, I spied the figure at the other end. I'd retained my weapon and held it out now so they could see it in my silhouette. Lightning flashed, illuminating our two figures on opposite sides of the roof, staring down one another. I saw now that the figure stood eye-to-eye with me, but spans apart, dressed in dark rain-soaked clothing. A heavy roll of thunder crashed around us.

"You've got nowhere to go," I shouted through the rain. "It's over."

The figure looked down the edge of the roofline toward the ground behind them, then back at me.

I steadied myself on the flattened portion of the narrow ridgeline. Wind swept up the shingles and threatened to blow me off my feet. I crouched low, trying not to look down, but couldn't help myself. I was unsteady on all fours and the roof was slippery. Rain continued to spatter around me as a flash lit up the house, the trees, and the bushes on the ground. In that split second, I spied a figure lurking in the cover of the tree line below. A hooded face stared up at me from the ground, features clear as day in the burst of lightning. Cho.

I almost lost what grip I had left. If Cho was down there, then who was up here? I glanced toward the darkened figure, who stood paralyzed with no place to go, then back to the trees. Cho was gone. She'd slipped away and taken the book with her. I wanted to cry. I was wet, I was cold, and now I'd failed Arthur.

But my fight wasn't over, and I choked back my tears and turned to my adversary on the roof. In a moment, the final puzzle piece had slipped into place. I now knew who stood before me, cold and shivering and cornered like a dog.

"Why did you do it?" I shouted. "You could have just moved on."

"He was going to take away my future," the figure shouted back. Swirls of rain mixed with wind carried the voice across the span between us.

"You didn't have to kill him." I steadied myself as I lifted back onto my feet. I inched along the roofline.

The figure searched frantically for a way off the roof—head turning this way and that, scanning for any leverage or foothold that would provide a viable escape. I continued my approach along the flat strip of roof, slowly closing the distance between us.

Finally choosing a way down, the shadow lowered itself off the end and dangled precariously over the lip of the roof. Only fingertips remained, struggling to hang on as I rushed forward as much as the wet conditions would allow. The knuckles turned white and pressed for more leverage. Just before I reached the edge to grasp an arm, the fingers slipped and disappeared from sight. A crash sounded below, followed by a squelch of guttural moaning.

I eased closer to the edge and peered over, not wanting to get too close myself. Another fit of lightning brought everything into a blaze of clarity. Below me lay Quentin, impaled on a discarded rusty pipe that stuck straight up from the dumpster. Rain splattered his face as life dripped away. A stream of blood, fed by the rain, poured from his gaping mouth.

I lay prostrate along the slender patch of roof, the fingers of one hand clutching the edge. I finally released the pipe from my grip and let it slide slowly down the wet tiles, bumping the cornice, and tumbling to the ground. I closed my eyes as blue flashing lights appeared and lit the surrounding treetops. All was silent—no rain, no thunder, no breathing. I hadn't even heard the siren as it pulled up to the house.

Twenty-three

THE SOFA SAGGED under the weight of the four of us—Harper, Angie, me, and Mayor Dewey—as we huddled together in a sort of emotional support group. I'd retreated off the roof somehow with only a few scrapes and bruises to show for my struggles. It was all still a blur, really. I remembered Harper and Angie's voices calling to me from below, then from the bedroom window, urging me back into the safety of the house.

The hours had gone by, sheriff personnel came and went, and the morning had chased away the storm. In these earliest hours of the day, the sun peeked over the horizon, glimmering through the tall windows that stretched high to the ceiling. Mayor Dewey had curled up in my lap, where he remained, napping while I'd shared what I'd seen that night with my friends. Cho had escaped and taken our book for whatever nefarious purpose she had planned.

Deputy Todd walked into the living room where we gathered, his boots echoing on the floor. "You've had a rough night, Miss Lewis," he said, taking a seat on my crate-table. "I can't fathom what possessed you to chase someone onto your roof in the middle of a lightning storm, but you seem to have a knack for getting into this kind of trouble."

"Deputy, I—"

"I'm not interested in your excuses, Miss Lewis. Not right now."

I hung my head and Angie squeezed my hand.

"What I *do* want to know," he continued, "is what in the world happened on your roof? And why another man is dead on your property."

"It was Quentin Qualls."

"Yes, we've established that," he said dryly.

I shook my head. "What I mean is, it was Quentin who killed Edgar."

"The apprentice?" Deputy Todd seemed doubtful. "How do you figure that?"

"I didn't really put it together until I was on the roof, staring at him, then it all sort of... fell into place."

Deputy Todd leaned back, but the crate threatened to topple over so he quickly corrected. "I'm not aware of any evidence that Quentin murdered Edgar, so you'll have to explain." He pulled out a notepad, ready to take down my words.

"It was really a combination of things," I said. "First, I don't think Quentin was a very good carpenter. Edgar had to correct what seemed like even the most basic of Quentin's carpentry work. Then Ryan—and he'll be so upset I said anything—Ryan had Quentin finish building a gazebo in his backyard. Except, when we sat on it, the whole thing broke apart. Pretty shoddy work."

"So, Quentin wasn't the greatest carpenter," said Harper. "How did you know he killed Edgar?"

"Things didn't add up when he asked Blister to take on his apprenticeship. You'll remember he was really close to taking his test?"

Angie and Harper nodded.

"Well, Blister was frustrated because it appeared that Edgar hadn't left any notes about the apprenticeship—no progress, no evaluations—all Blister had to go on was what Quentin could provide him."

"That's convenient," said Harper.

"Exactly. But it was also out of character for Edgar. At least a few people mentioned that Edgar kept meticulous records—so why would those records go missing?"

"You think Quentin did something to Edgar's records?"

"I suspect so, yes. I'd bet Edgar wasn't going to approve him to move on in the apprenticeship—or was going to cancel it altogether—and Quentin, after putting in all those years, couldn't let that happen."

"I'd be pretty upset, too," Harper said, "if the last few years of my life were about to be put down the drain."

Deputy Todd held up his hand. "Hold on, you're telling me that Quentin killed Edgar in order to trick Blister into taking on his apprenticeship so he could coast to the end of it?"

"That's about right. Blister was so nice, gullible even—sorry Angie—and he felt so bad about Quentin losing his apprenticeship so close to completion, that he jumped at the chance to help poor Quentin finish it out."

"With as few records of his true skill and ability as

possible," added Harper.

"But why was Edgar found in your bedroom?" asked Angie. "That doesn't make any sense."

"Dimitri told me he heard footsteps while he was locked in the upstairs bathroom. I think he heard Quentin and Edgar going up the stairs. Quentin may have lured him there for what he thought was enough privacy to do the deed."

"That's quite a leap of logic, Miss Lewis," said Deputy Todd.

I nodded. "I know, and I wasn't really sure until tonight, when we planted the fake clue."

"Fake clue?" Deputy Todd eyed us suspiciously.

Harper waved him off. "Long story. Keep going, Poppy."

"I hate to say it, but I really thought the murderer could still have been either Maisie, Cho, or Quentin. But Maisie's too short—I knew right away that the intruder tonight wasn't her."

"And Cho?" Deputy Todd asked.

"She…" Angie and Harper hugged me tighter. They knew I didn't want to say too much about Cho to Deputy Todd. The events of that night had unfolded so quickly, it hadn't occurred to me at the time, but it was obvious now. My own actions seemed reckless in hindsight. "She wouldn't have gone out on the roof in an electrical storm. She's too aware of the danger and would have found any other way to escape if it were her."

Deputy Todd considered this explanation for a moment and finally nodded. "Sounds like a tragic story," he said, standing up. "The cleanup's done here, so why don't you all get some rest."

"Thanks, deputy," said Angie. "We'll take care of her."

Harper walked Deputy Todd to the door and returned with the morning newspaper. She held it up for Angie and me to see. "Well, we made the front page."

There was the headline, in big bold letters at the top, clear as day for all to read.

Dewey Defeats Thornen

"At least it will be news for a day," Harper continued. "Tomorrow's paper will be full of this drama."

"Sorry, Harper," I said. She'd worked so hard for this moment. The newspaper article was a validation for her, and now it would be fleeting.

But Harper just shrugged. "It's all right. Being mayor can't be all parties and cat toys. It was fun while it lasted."

Angie and I shared a quick glance.

"You can't expect Mayor Dewey to—"

A loud knock at the door cut Angie off.

"Probably just Deputy Todd back for something else." We eased ourselves up from the sofa as the knocking came again.

"I'm coming, Deputy," I shouted.

But as I opened the door, I wasn't greeted by our deputy. It was Greta, staring up at me, a sly grin spread across her face. Harper and Angie quickly came up beside me at the door. Angie clutched my arm, finally laying eyes on the woman we'd told her about.

"What do you want?" Harper demanded.

Greta paid her no mind and continued to stare directly into my eyes, unblinking. "You saw her. Now you believe."

After a moment I slowly nodded, then stepped back from the doorway, making room for the old woman to come through. Harper and Angie glanced at me from either side then also moved out of the way. "All right, Greta," I said, continuing to stare at her as she stepped inside. "Tell us everything you know."

The End of Book 2

Lucinda Harrison is a writer and crafter who lives in northern California with her two mischievous cats. She is the author of the Poppy Lewis Mystery series.

Connect online at lucindaharrisonauthor.com

OTHER BOOKS BY LUCINDA HARRISON

Poppy Lewis Mystery Series
Murder in Starry Cove

Made in the USA
Monee, IL
20 June 2021